Promise the Night

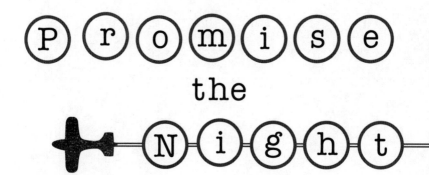

Promise the Night

A NOVEL — by *Michaela MacColl*

chronicle books · san francisco

To Mom, a fearless pilot and terrific lady. You inspired this book.

Library of Congress Cataloging-in-Publication Data

MacColl, Michaela.
  Promise the night / by Michaela MacColl.
     p. cm.
  Summary: Explores the early life of Beryl Markham, who grew up on a farm
in Kenya, and became the first person to fly solo across the Atlantic from east
to west.
  ISBN 978-0-8118-7625-4 (alk. paper)
  1. Markham, Beryl—Juvenile fiction. 2. Markham, Beryl—Childhood and
youth—Juvenile fiction. 3. Women air pilots—Kenya—Juvenile fiction. 4. Women
air pilots—Great Britain—Juvenile fiction. 5. Kenya—History—1895–1963—
Fiction. [1. Markham, Beryl—Childhood and youth—Fiction. 2. Air pilots—Fiction.
3. Kenya—History—1895–1963—Fiction.] I. Title.
  PZ7.M13384Ps 2011
  813.6—dc22

                                       2011010938

Book design by Jennifer Tolo Pierce.
Typeset in Adobe Caslon, ITC American Typewriter, and Ruly.

Manufactured in China.

10 9 8 7 6 5 4 3 2 1

Chronicle Books LLC
680 Second Street, San Francisco, California 94107

www.chroniclekids.com

BERYL MARKHAM

The Daily Express
19 August, 1936
London, England

I am going to set out to fly the Atlantic to New York. Not as a society girl. Not as a woman even. But as a pilot with two thousand flying hours, mostly in uncharted Africa, to my credit. The only thing that really counts is whether one can fly. I have a license. I can take an engine apart and put it back. I can navigate. I am fit and given ordinary luck I am sure I can fly to New York.

This is to be no stunt flight. No woman's superiority-over-man affair. I don't want to be superior to men. If I can be a good pilot, I'll be the happiest creature alive.

CHAPTER ONE

1912, Green Hills Farm, Njoro, British East Africa (present-day Kenya)

BERYL SAT BOLT UPRIGHT, HER HEART BEATING FASTER. ALONE in her mud hut at night, she expected to hear certain noises: the rustling of insects burrowing in the thatch roof, the snorting of the horses, and sometimes even the roar of a lion in the valley. But these ordinary noises had suddenly stopped.

"Buller, did you hear something?" she whispered. The only answer in the darkness was her dog's snore from the polished mud floor of her hut. "Some watchdog you are!"

Holding her breath, she listened carefully. Beryl ran her hand under her monkey-skin bedspread, searching for her trusty "bushman's friend." Taken secretly from her father's hut, the vicious blade was sharp enough to deal with anything.

Brushing the mosquito netting aside, she swung her legs off the bed and crept to the door. The only thing between her and the night was a thick burlap sack secured to the door frame with leather ties. She tugged the ties open, drew back the rough cloth, and slipped outside. With a heavy sigh, Buller lumbered to his feet and joined her.

The cold clear air drove away her drowsiness. Dressed only in one of her father's old nightshirts, she shivered as the chill sliced through the fine linen. The moon was just rising, illuminating the vast valley dropping away at her feet.

Beryl turned toward the pitch-black forest behind her. She stared long enough for the trees to take individual shape. Her father had forbidden her to go into the forest alone. Any danger would come from there.

Buller lifted his head and sniffed. He whined deep in his throat.

"What do you smell, boy?" Beryl asked. She tried sniffing, too, but inhaling the cold air burned her nostrils. She glanced over at her father's *rondavel* twenty yards away. Like her hut, it was covered with a thick straw roof. Until the big house was finished, her father's house was as tiny as hers. Most settlers slept in their own huts; the mud buildings were quick to build and lasted for years.

A thin line of light illuminated the sacking of her father's window. He would be doing the accounts. By day, he drove himself and his men to exhaustion. At night, he tried to make the Green Hills farm profitable by writing numbers in different columns. He would be furious if she interrupted his work to report an unusual silence.

Beryl took one last hard look around. She didn't see anything, but her father always said that what you don't notice in Africa can get you killed. Glancing into the clear sky, she saw Orion, the hunter, outlined in the stars. He was an old friend. Her view was blocked by an owl, wings extended, who glided above her head with a soft hoot before disappearing into the valley. What must it be like to soar over the trees and meadows—to see Africa from up high? To be afraid of nothing? To be able to see danger in the dark, not just have vague worries about strange silences?

She slipped back into the safety of her hut, ducking under the burlap door. Buller lay down in his usual spot at the end of the bed. The day after her mother had abandoned Beryl and her father, Beryl had persuaded Buller to sleep with her in the tiny hut. He was as unlike Mama as it was possible to be. She was aristocratic and beautiful. Buller was an ugly mutt, a mix of bull terrier and sheepdog. But while Mama had left Africa without a backward glance, Buller was still her loyal friend who never left Beryl's side.

Daddy said Mama left because the size of Africa frightened her. And she wanted indoor plumbing. Beryl could no longer remember her mother's face, but the sting of her mother not asking Beryl to go with her still smarted. Nevertheless, she managed just fine: alone with her father, Buller, the horses, and Africa, with the nearest neighbor miles away.

Beryl threw herself into bed, tucking the mosquito netting around her body. Holding her knife tightly, she stared into the darkness, listening hard and pinching herself to keep awake.

Later, when it was all over, she wondered what would have happened if she had remembered to tie down the burlap door. If she had not been so careless, would the danger have passed her by?

Her only warning was a patch of lighter night by the door. The leopard must have slunk in, crawling soundlessly on his stomach the way cats do. Ears flat to his head. Spotted fur standing up on his back. Eyes fixed on his prey. Waiting. Waiting . . .

Buller's anguished yelp filled the hut. When she heard the deep yowl, she knew it was a cat, probably a leopard. Beryl huddled beneath the safety of the mosquito netting, afraid the cat would finish off Buller and then go after her.

"Buller! Be careful, boy!" Beryl screamed at the top of her voice. She waved the knife in the dark. She couldn't see what was happening, but she could hear Buller's low growl. She imagined that the leopard was poised to spring onto her bed.

"Daddy!" she cried. She ripped off the blanket and snapped it toward the battling animals. Even if she had the courage, Beryl knew she shouldn't join the fight on the floor; she was just as likely to hurt Buller as help him.

Beryl could make out the leopard's shadow, spotted even in the dimness. It sprang onto Buller's back and sank its sharp teeth in the loose skin at the back of his neck.

"DADDY!"

Beryl heard what sounded like Buller's back cracking as he tried to shake off the cat. Before she could scream again, the leopard had dragged her friend out of her *rondavel*. Buller's cries ended as suddenly as they began.

She leapt out of bed and ran into the bulk of her father; he was in the doorway, carrying a hurricane lamp.

"Beryl! Are you hurt?" He ran his hands lightly over her head and body, as if checking the soundness of one of his thoroughbreds. "What happened?"

"A leopard got into the hut."

"What? Where?"

"It's gone—he took Buller!" A sob escaped her. "Daddy, Buller's hurt. We have to go get him."

"Be quiet, Beryl. Crying won't help him now." He stood up and cast the lantern's light around the room. "Let me look."

He knelt to the floor and touched a spot. He brought his finger to his nose. "Blood. Whether Buller's or the cat's, I don't know." He glanced around. "How did he get in? Didn't you close the door?"

She closed her eyes and sobbed. "It's all my fault, Daddy!"

"Beryl . . . stop caterwauling. Answer me. What happened?" The lamp cast a ghostly light on the sharp planes of his face. His gray eyes were unyielding.

"I got up in the night, Daddy," she admitted. "I forgot to tie the door down."

"How many times have I told you?" He shrugged. "Careless."

"I'm sorry, Daddy."

"It's a hard way to learn your lesson." He shook his head, and the lines of his face softened just a bit.

"Daddy, we have to find Buller and save him." Tears streamed from her eyes. "Please help me, Daddy."

Her father stared at the pool of blood on the floor of her hut. He didn't answer.

"Please, Daddy. Please." Clutching her knife in one hand, she grabbed her father's hand and squeezed hard with the other.

"Where did you get that knife?" he asked.

"I don't remember," she said, not meeting his eyes. "Come on, Daddy. We have to save Buller."

He shook his head. "Beryl, it's too late. Either the dog will survive or it won't."

Beryl didn't say a word, but her whole body trembled with pleading.

"Don't look like that," he said with irritation. "A farmer's daughter can't afford to be sentimental about animals."

"Please . . ." Her words came out in a croak. "Buller was Mama's dog."

"Oh, for pity's sake," he burst out. He pulled his hand away and wiped his brow. "Get your boots on and we'll take a look around. But it's probably a wasted effort."

Biting her lip to keep from crying, Beryl pulled on her boots. She followed her father into the compound as he tracked the spots of blood into the forest by the light of his lantern. There was so much of it—on the leaves of bushes, in pools on the ground. Wherever they followed the blood trace, the forest was silent, as though all the animals and night insects were holding their breath. The nest of ancient trees and vines was even more ominous at night.

After a few hundred yards, they lost the trail.

"Beryl, there's nothing we can do."

"I'm sure he's around here somewhere," Beryl insisted. "I think I hear him."

Holding the lantern above their heads, her father placed a hand on her shoulder. "Even if Buller fought back, he's badly wounded. False hope is worse than no hope at all, Beryl. Especially in Africa."

"But . . ."

"No buts. If I have time tomorrow, we'll look again, but Buller's almost certainly dead. I'll get you a new dog."

"But . . ."

"Not another word, young lady. And you'll sleep in my hut the rest of the night. I don't trust you to be sensible." He turned and began the trek back to their small compound of huts. Dashing the tears from her cheeks, Beryl cast a last look into the undergrowth.

"Don't die, Buller. I'll come for you," she promised into the darkness.

NEWS CHRONICLE

LONDON, ENGLAND   3 SEPTEMBER, 1936

EDITORIAL

We hope Mrs. Beryl Markham will never take off. The time for these "pioneer" solo flights in overloaded radio-less machines has passed. . . . If she came down in the ocean she would cause prolonged suspense to all her friends and considerable inconvenience and expense to all the ships who would have to search for her. We hope that Mrs. Markham will think better of it.

CHAPTER TWO

EYES SQUEEZED SHUT, BERYL LISTENED TO THE NOISES OF HER father getting ready for the morning. She lay perfectly still until she heard his voice outside, berating the workers in his British-accented Swahili. As she swung her legs off the extra cot in his hut, a furry, bony hand grabbed her ankle. She stifled a scream.

"Simi, you are the most useless pet." She kicked at the baboon and chased him back under the bed, a favorite hiding place. "I don't know why Daddy doesn't just skin you for a blanket. Buller is worth a hundred of you."

She pulled on her usual clothes: a man's shirt tucked inside a pair of khaki shorts cinched tight with one of her father's belts. For warmth, she tied a blanket around her shoulders. She pulled on her boots and strapped her father's machete to her belt. Its long blade was useful to clear underbrush, but she had another use for it today. If she found that leopard, she would need more than her little knife to protect herself.

Opening the door slowly, so as not to attract attention, she was relieved to see her father striding down to the stables, barking out orders. She hugged the outer wall of the hut until she was out of sight and headed into the woods.

The forest was forbidden territory. Her father would be furious. She glanced back; she could still see the huts of the farm behind her. But after a few more steps, the shadowy trees and dense underbrush engulfed her.

It was easy enough to find their path from the night before, because the leaves were still bruised. She followed the trail deeper into the forest until she reached a small clearing and the blood trail disappeared. All around her, she heard the forest beginning to stir. She didn't know where to go next.

The chittering of the monkeys mocked her failure.

Into the glade, she whispered, "Buller, I'm sorry. I was stupid. Stupid. Stupid."

The sun rose higher and the night shadows receded. She would have to return before her father noticed she was gone. But how could she go back without Buller? She perched on a rotten tree trunk and sank her head in her hands.

The hairs on the back of her neck began to tingle. Something was watching her. Had the leopard come for her? She lifted her head slowly and peeked through her fingers. Standing at the edge of the clearing, not ten feet from her, was a native boy. She'd often watched packs of boys like this marching on the road. The red cloth of his *shuka*, the toga the natives wore, was a like a splash of blood against the green leaves.

Beryl swallowed hard, dropped a hand to her machete, and forced herself to look him straight in the eye. His face looked as if it was chiseled in polished black stone. A fluttering of a startled bird in the underbrush made her suddenly appreciate how far she was from home.

"Who are you?" she asked.

The boy stepped into the clearing, a patch of light shining on his shaved skull. He stared at her and shook his head quizzically.

Beryl switched to Swahili, a language she had spoken since she was a toddler. "Why do you spy on me?"

He answered, "I am not spying. I am looking for a foolish white girl who has gotten lost in the forest."

He was about the same age as she, Beryl realized, and her fear left as quickly as it had arrived. "Then you must be looking for someone else, because I'm not lost. I'm looking for my dog."

"Why was your head in your hands?" he asked. "Is your dog hiding there?"

"I'm thinking. You wouldn't understand."

Suddenly he grinned, and his bright white teeth transformed his face into that of a possible ally.

"My name is Kibii. I am from the Nandi tribe," he said.

"Beryl," she answered with a small smile of her own. "I'm British."

His mouth shaped the unfamiliar name and he tried a few times to pronounce it. "I'll call you Beru," he said finally. "You are the daughter of the Captain; he said your hair was the color of a lion." He reached over and with one finger touched her hair, which lay wild and tangled around her shoulders. Beryl didn't flinch;

ever since she could remember, Africans had wanted to touch her blond hair.

"My father sent you?" she asked.

"He said you were in the woods, even though he had forbidden you to go. It was Arap Maina who sent me to find you."

"Who is Arap Maina?" she asked.

"My father. He has come to work for your father, Captain Cluttabucki."

"Clutterbuck," Beryl corrected. "How did you find me?" If Kibii had found her so easily, perhaps he could help her track Buller.

"You left a trail like a wounded warthog." Kibii stood even taller. "I am a hunter."

"Can you find my dog? A leopard took him last night."

"It happens." The boy shrugged. "But it is only a dog. In my village, we have many dogs."

"Buller is not just a dog," Beryl said. "He is my only friend."

The boy looked at her for a long time without blinking. "Then I will find him," he said finally. "You lost the trail here?" he asked, looking carefully around the clearing.

Beryl nodded. Kibii headed into the underbrush for about ten yards. Beryl stood up and brushed the bits of rotten tree from her shorts. Remembering what her father had said, she didn't dare hope too much. She spoke to his back. "Do you see anything?"

"Ssshh," Kibii said, without looking at her. "You talk too much." He began moving about the forest, spiraling out from their starting point in wider circles.

"Blood," he said, showing her a speck on the ground. He loped into the forest, his feet making no sound. Beryl followed as best she could.

He finally paused along a stream. "I have heard elephants that run more quietly," he said, frowning. "A hunter as loud as you would starve."

Beryl could feel her face redden, like a sunburn. "I've never hunted," she admitted.

"Of course not. You are a girl," he said. He knelt down and touched an area of churned-up mud. "That is your leopard. He is still dragging your friend." He seemed to read the ground as easily as Beryl's father read the racing forms.

Kibii followed the stream and Beryl trailed behind him. She looked around curiously; she had never been this deep in the forest. Brightly colored birds flew out of the bushes, cawing loudly. A stick cracked. She whirled around to face . . . nothing.

"Beru, we are close," Kibii said, brushing aside tree branches overhanging the water. "Here!"

"Buller!"

The dog lay on his side in the mud, his snout near the water's edge. His jaw was pierced through. Beryl guessed the leopard had tried to crack it in two with its sharp teeth. There were long gashes in his black-and-white coat, and his fur was caked with blood. He wasn't moving.

"He's dead!" Beryl cried.

Kibii shook his head. "The dead don't bleed," he said, pointing to the blood oozing from a cut on Buller's cheek.

The dog's eyes flickered open and his tail thumped weakly. His eyes closed again. Dashing away her tears, Beryl closed her own eyes in thanks.

"His injuries are very bad." Kibii shook his head. "You should kill him now—he would suffer less."

"Buller is tough," Beryl said, her voice trembling. She cleared her throat and began again. "Help me save him." Scooping water in her hand, she began to wash away some of the dried blood from the dog's snout.

"It is a waste of time," Kibii said.

"Kibii, please." She laid her hand on his forearm. He started, like one of her father's horses when a fly landed on its flank, but then he relaxed.

"Wait here." He was swallowed up by the thick underbrush in seconds.

Beryl cradled Buller's head in her lap and stroked his favorite spot behind his ears. He moaned, and for the first time Beryl knew the sound of agony. "It's all right, boy," she said. "Hold on."

The forest seemed suddenly quiet. She looked at the thick greenery that surrounded them as far as she could see. What if Kibii didn't return? She couldn't get Buller home alone. But no sooner did she doubt him than Kibii emerged from the underbrush, holding a bunch of green leaves.

"What is that?" she asked.

"My father taught me healing. This plant is good *dawa*," he said. She nodded. "Good medicine."

He packed Buller's worst wounds with the leaves. Then he pulled Beryl's blanket from around her shoulders and wrapped it around the dog. With deft hands, he fashioned a sling so that he and Beryl could share the burden. Beryl watched with growing admiration; he had skills she had only dreamed about. Sweating in her thin shirt, she staggered as she helped Kibii carry Buller's sixty pounds out of the forest.

"Hold on, boy," she whispered.

Kibii, in the lead, glanced back, but didn't say a word. She wondered if he understood any English.

Beryl had completely lost her bearings, so when they emerged from the forest she was startled to see her father's compound only a few hundred yards away.

"Quick!" she said. "To my hut. We can get Buller inside before Daddy sees us."

But they had covered only half the distance to the hut when they heard an angry voice.

"It's my father," Beryl said.

"And mine." Kibii stopped dead in his tracks, forcing Beryl to do the same.

Buller whimpered. Beryl took a firmer grip on the sling.

The Captain, who was of modest height, looked taller as he strode over. Beneath his short-cropped hair, his face was red with anger. "Beryl Clutterbuck, I'll have your hide for this."

Following him was an African man who looked like a grown-up version of Kibii. He was tall and thin, with skin like polished leather. Unlike Kibii's, his skull was wrinkled. A *shuka* was draped elegantly around his body. He wore dozens of necklaces made of wire, and earrings that dangled down to his shoulders. Around his upper arms, iron bracelets pressed into his skin.

"Daddy, we found Buller!" Beryl said.

"Did I not forbid you to go in the forest alone?" her father asked.

"I know, but Buller . . ."

"No buts. Do you have any idea how dangerous it is out there?" With his thumb and forefinger, he rubbed the bridge of his nose. Beryl was startled to see how tired he looked. "I don't have time to worry about you gallivanting in the woods."

"But we found him! I couldn't follow the trail, but then Kibii helped . . ."

Her father's fists clenched and unclenched as though he were just keeping from striking her. Beryl fell silent.

"How badly hurt is he?" he asked. "Because it would be just like you to risk your life for a lost cause." He unfolded a bit of cloth and looked at Buller's injuries. He whistled under his breath. "I've half a mind to put him down, just to teach you a lesson."

Beryl gulped. She stared at her father and hoped the tears would stay behind her eyes; the Captain hated weakness. Only strength could save Buller now.

Kibii whispered to his father in a rapid language Beryl couldn't quite understand. Arap Maina stepped forward. "May I look at the animal, Captain?" he asked, very respectfully.

The Captain gave permission in his clipped Swahili. "Go ahead, Arap Maina. I think it is hopeless, but my daughter loves the animal."

Beryl and Kibii lay Buller on the ground. Beryl held her breath as Arap Maina checked the wounds. He straightened up and faced Captain Clutterbuck.

"Sahib, with care, the dog will live. Your daughter need not be sad."

Beryl exhaled.

"Good, she can take him with her to England," the Captain said. He held up a hand to stop Beryl's howl of protest. "Beryl," he said in English, "if you keep running wild, you're going to get yourself killed."

"I want to stay here with you," she pleaded. "You need me. I'm your best stable lad. Who else can ride like me?"

"I can't run the farm and keep you out of trouble at the same time." He was implacable.

"But Daddy, this is my home. Please don't make me go . . ."

Kibii whispered to his father again and Arap Maina interrupted Beryl's pleas. "Sahib, perhaps I can care for your daughter?"

"You were hired to supervise the men," the Captain said with a frown. "Not to be a blasted nanny to a little girl."

"I'm nearly eleven!" Beryl fell silent at her father's look.

"I have come here to work," said Arap Maina, "but also to teach the *totos*, the children of the tribe, the ways of the Nandi. I can teach your daughter as well."

"Daddy, I'd be safe with him. You wouldn't have to worry anymore." Beryl wanted to jump up and down with excitement, but she dared not fidget while her father considered Arap Maina's offer.

"She wouldn't be a nuisance?" her father asked slowly.

"No, sahib. The children of our tribe are just as likely to get into trouble." Arap Maina glared at Kibii, who dared to laugh. "My son says she has the tread of a water buffalo, but she learns quickly. And she is a loyal friend."

The Captain stared at Beryl, taking in the bloodstained shirt and the cuts and scratches on her bare legs. "Arap Maina, I accept your offer. Since her mother left, she has been nothing but a worry to me."

Beryl's heart suddenly felt like lead. Her father's thoughts and eyes were already wandering down the hill, where the gristmill was.

Half the farm's income came from grinding maize, but Beryl could see the wheel had stopped. The native workers were beginning to drift away to other tasks.

The Captain pulled out his pocket watch and made an impatient noise against his teeth. To Beryl, he said, "Young lady, Arap Maina is a warrior and important in his tribe. Don't give him any trouble. I need his men to work the farm."

"Yes, Daddy."

"And take care of that damned dog." Shaking his head, he returned to the business of farming.

Beryl watched her father walk away. She took her eyes off his back only when Arap Maina began to speak. "We must consider this leopard who comes into Cluttabucki's daughter's house. He is too bold."

Beryl nodded, although his words made her nervous. She knew firsthand how fierce that leopard was.

He continued, "But for today, Kibii will show you how we heal our animals."

Kibii stood up even straighter, a wide smile on his face.

"And perhaps tomorrow you can visit our village and meet the other *totos*."

Beryl could barely say a word. Her day had started with nothing. But now she had her dog, a teacher, and a friend.

By the time I was twenty-six, I was not only the first woman racehorse trainer, I was one of the most successful in Africa. The life and job had been enough for my father, and I always thought it would content me as well. Until I saw an airplane.

There weren't many planes yet in Africa. Something about the preposterous combination of combustion engines and wings stirred my imagination. One day some friends brought me to the Nairobi airstrip, such as it was, to see a plane land. The flying machine had to circle half a dozen times until the zebras and the wildebeests were chased off the runway.

The pilot's name was Tom Black. We got to talking about flying. Tom wanted to start a business delivering mail and medical supplies to villages so remote they weren't on any map. He said that even if Africa didn't have roads, there was land enough for the wheels of planes, and sky enough for their wings.

That night, I went back to the stable and said to Arap Ruta, my head lad and good friend, "I think I am going to leave all this and learn to fly." Arap Ruta stood in a loose box beside a freshly groomed colt whose coat gleamed like light on water. He shrugged and dusted his hands, one against the other.

"If it is to be that we must fly, memsahib, then we will fly. At what hour of the morning do we begin?"

Simple as that, I left my old life behind and began a new adventure.

CHAPTER THREE

EVER SINCE ARAP MAINA'S INVITATION, BERYL COULD THINK OF nothing but her visit to the Nandi village. Except Buller, of course, who at that moment was snoring next to her bed. In his sleep, he would sometimes roll over on his wounds, groan, and roll back with a whimper. But he was alive and on the mend.

"Get some rest, boy," she said, checking his bandages. "I'll tell you all about it when I get back."

Beryl's fingers trembled as she twisted her tangled hair into two loose braids. Something was beginning; she was sure of it. She donned shirt, shorts, and boots, and she was ready to go. The rim of the horizon was just glowing with the sunrise as she untied the door and found Kibii already waiting. He stood on one leg, the other folded behind his back, like an exotic bird. Beryl noticed his footprint in the damp earth. Although her breath hung on the chill morning air, she knew that the sun would soon steam the moisture away.

Kibii frowned. "Finally," he said.

"Your father said at daybreak." Beryl pursed her lips. "Have you been wasting time waiting for me?"

He grinned. "How is your dog?"

"Buller is well."

He nodded. "Follow me."

Kibii loped toward the edge of the farm, where the path dropped into the deep valley. Beryl hesitated. She was not allowed to go into the valley alone.

Kibii was already far ahead, weaving through the tall grass. He stopped and waved his arm wide to hurry her up. Eyes fixed on his back, Beryl pushed herself to run as quickly and confidently as Kibii.

"I'm coming," Beryl called as she ran, dodging the waist-high anthills. In passing, she touched one; the ants swarmed away from her hands. The hill was hard as a rock.

"You are too slow," Kibii complained, "and easily distracted."

"Once your father trains me, I'll get better," she panted, catching up to him.

Kibii put out his hand to stop her in her tracks. "Sssshh."

A wildebeest crashed through the underbrush across the path.

"How did you know it was coming?" Beryl asked. "I didn't hear a thing."

"Because you were talking." Kibii removed his hand. "Girls always talk. It is why they don't hunt."

"That's a lie." Beryl drew herself up and stared Kibii in the face. "I don't talk too much."

"Because you have no one to talk to." Kibii smiled smugly. "When you meet my father's wives and my sisters, you will chatter just like them."

The path corkscrewed down the hill. A sharp turn, and suddenly there was a vicious-looking fence made of acacia branches, the thorns facing outward. A dozen round huts made of mud and sticks were tucked inside the fence. To one side was a paddock filled with dark-colored cattle, lowing gently. Beryl noticed that half the huts still needed roofs; but for that, she would have thought the houses had always been part of the landscape. "How long have you been here?" she asked.

He shrugged. "Not long."

"You should come help my father with his new house. He's been building it for months and it's still not done."

Kibii led the way through a gap in the thorn fence. He stopped to admire a young bull with distinctive white splotches and a fine set of horns.

"That one is mine. Last year, I was wrestling Mehru when I was supposed to mind the herd. This calf wandered away. I was afraid to come home, so I hid in a tree for two days. But my father had already found him. When I came home, he gave the calf to me."

Beryl's mouth dropped open. "You were careless; you should have been punished."

"I had punished myself already. And my father knew that if one of the cattle was mine, I would guard the rest more carefully."

"My father would never give me a foal because I lost a horse," she said.

Kibii shrugged and rubbed his bull's nose.

"Your cattle are very fine," Beryl said politely.

Kibii's chest swelled with pride. "This is our tribe's wealth."

"My father has twelve horses, but we'll get more as soon as he can afford to import more bloodstock."

"I have never seen anything like your father's horses," Kibii said. "They are not like zebras."

"Of course not," Beryl answered with scorn. "Zebras are useless."

"Can you eat your horses?"

Beryl was horrified. "Of course not!"

"Can you milk them?"

"Don't be ridiculous!" Beryl snorted.

"Then what use are they?"

"When you ride a racehorse, you feel like you are flying," Beryl said simply.

Kibii was still for a moment. "You can ride?"

"Yes, of course." Beryl's shoulders went back and her chin tilted up; finally there was something she could do that Kibii couldn't.

"Then I will ride horses, too."

"Riding is harder than it looks," Beryl warned. "But if you teach me how to track animals, I'll teach you to ride."

"Agreed."

Kibii picked an insect out of the corner of his bull's eye. The beast lowed, but did not move.

"He trusts you," Beryl said.

"Of course he does."

"How many cows does your family have?" Beryl asked.

"Well," Kibii looked thoughtful. "There is Mongo and Nure and Muge and . . ."

Beryl laughed. "But how many do you have?"

"Beru, it is greedy to count cattle." Beryl jumped at the sound of Arap Maina's voice behind her. "It is enough to know the name of every cow and bull. The boys of the tribe would know if one were missing."

Every Englishman Beryl had ever met judged his wealth by counting it. But now that she thought about it, her father's horses all had names and personalities. One stallion could sire a whole line of racehorses. What did it matter how many more you had?

"Arap Maina, I am here to start my training," she said.

His dark eyes stared at her, unblinking. Today he wore even more necklaces, made of fine wire threaded with colored beads and the odd English coin, piled one upon another. Beryl wondered that he didn't stoop under the weight of them.

As the silence lengthened, she wondered what to say next. Before she could decide, two women, one old and one young, stepped out of the nearest hut. Their heads were shaved, showing off their high foreheads and earrings in the upper part of their ears as well as in the lobes. Beryl peered behind them, but couldn't see anything inside the hut except blue smoke. A bleating goat ran to Kibii and licked his knee. The older woman made a clucking noise and it scampered back inside.

"This is my mother, Namasari," Kibii said, gesturing to the older woman. She nodded, her face wary. Namasari's skull was lined with deep wrinkles, and her collarbones jutted up through her coils of necklaces. "This is my other mother, Naipende."

Arap Maina's second wife was much younger than his first, and very beautiful. She wore a skirt of monkey skins that reached to her ankles, and her broad smile reached her eyes.

"Hello," Beryl said quietly.

"Welcome," said Naipende.

A young girl, perhaps a year or two older than Beryl, emerged from the gloomy hut. Her face was round, and her lips were as full as her figure. She watched Beryl with ill-disguised hostility.

Beryl lifted her chin and stared back.

"My sister, Jebbta," Kibii said.

Arap Maina said to Kibii, "Join the other *totos* while I talk to Beru. They are practicing with their spears."

Beryl stepped forward. "I would like to learn how to do that."

Arap Maina's forehead creased in the slightest frown. "Beru, your father asked that you learn our ways. And you shall." He took her hand and tied a leather bracelet with a shell around her wrist. "This says you are a girl of our tribe. You are part of our family."

Beryl fingered the bracelet, wondering which ocean had tossed up this shell. The British East African colony was filled with people from all over the world; it could be from anywhere. "Thank you, Arap Maina. I will treasure it always."

"Today, the women and girls will be weaving the roofs for our new homes. My wives will show you how." Both women nodded.

Beryl couldn't believe her ears. "You want me to thatch roofs?"

"You said you wished to be part of our tribe." Arap Maina was puzzled. "This is what the girls do."

"We weave reeds and grasses," Naipende said helpfully. "It makes a very good roof. Very dry."

"But ... I thought I was going to learn how to hunt," Beryl said.

Everyone burst out laughing except Arap Maina, who looked thoughtful.

"You are only a girl, like me," Jebbta said.

"Men hunt and fight," Kibii said. "Women build the houses, gather the firewood, and cook. And take care of the babies."

"I don't care about those things—I want to learn to hunt!"

"Why?" Arap Maina's question was neutral.

"To kill the leopard that hurt my dog." Even as she said it, Beryl knew that this was not enough.

"We do not hunt for revenge," Arap Maina said. "We hunt to protect the herd."

Feeling her dream slip away, Beryl argued, "You said the leopard was too bold. My father's horses need to be protected."

"I will kill the leopard," said Arap Maina. "You will work with the women."

"But ... I can do anything Kibii can do." Beryl felt the tears welling up in her eyes.

"You see," Kibii crowed, "girls cry. Boys never cry."

Beryl squeezed her eyes to stop the tears. "I'm not crying," she said.

Arap Maina's face was like the anthill; hard as rock, but with much activity inside. "Beru, if you want me to teach you, first you must learn to obey."

"But my father told you ..."

"I offered to teach you like the children of the tribe. If you refuse to learn what I wish to teach, your father will have to accept that."

"What if he does not accept it?" Beryl knew she was making a threat her father would never honor.

"Then . . ." Arap Maina shrugged, his face patient.

"Then what?" she asked, worried she had gone too far.

"We will leave."

"I don't want you to go," cried Beryl. She clenched the shell so hard it cut into her palm.

Arap Maina waited, perfectly still.

Beryl looked at the unfinished roof. The completed portion looked more compact and sturdy than her own. Maybe she could make her roof a bit drier. "If I do this, can I learn to hunt?"

"Beru, everything we learn today prepares us for tomorrow."

Grinding the traces of tears into her cheeks with the palm of her hand, Beryl sniffed. "So tomorrow I can hunt?"

Arap Maina and the others burst out laughing. Without a word, Beryl gathered up armfuls of the sharp branches to use as thatch. After all, Arap Maina hadn't said no.

I was flying my little two-seater around British East Africa, shuttling mail and medical patients to places that weren't on any maps. I was one of just a few women in the world with a commercial pilot's license. Although I was making a good living, I wanted to make a lot more money. My friend Blix was a big game hunter. He took rich men out to the bush to hunt elephants for the ivory. We had the idea that I could help with my little plane. I believe I was the first person to ever scout elephants by plane.

Tom Black heard about it and told me it was sheer madness and bloody dangerous. He was right, of course. There weren't any runways out there, except what the expedition carved out of the bush. And even if you made the landing, that was no guarantee that you would have enough room to take off again. There was no radio if you got in trouble. And if you were unlucky enough to be stranded out there, there were wild animals, dysentery, tsetse flies, and, worst of all, the *siafu* ants. I carried a vial of morphine and a pistol, just in case. It wasn't sensible. Maybe that's why I loved it.

CHAPTER FOUR

BERYL HAD TO AGREE WITH THE NANDI WOMEN; SHE WAS A complete failure as a young girl of the tribe. Not that she wasn't trying, she explained to Arap Maina, it was just that weaving, cooking, and minding little children bored her. After several weeks, Arap Maina relented and let Beryl train with the boys. She learned to track animals, wrestle, and even throw a spear at a target. But Arap Maina still refused to let her hunt.

One morning, however, training was suspended because Captain Clutterbuck needed them to meet the train at Nakuru, the makeshift town five miles south of Green Hills farm, and the train's last stop. Arap Maina, Kibii, and Beryl stood apart from the group of dusty settlers. The train brought the post, news, and basic necessities from Nairobi, a hundred miles to the east. Everyone had been waiting since midmorning, wilting in the scorching heat.

"When will the train come?" Kibii asked. He carefully pronounced the word "train" because Beryl wouldn't let him call it an "iron snake" as the other Africans did.

"It breaks down all the time," Beryl explained. "Usually at the steepest part of the hill. Then all the passengers get off and walk."

Kibii snorted. "Do they know it is lion country?"

Beryl shrugged. People coming up here should know the dangers, but many ignored them.

Beryl plucked her sweat-soaked shirt away from her body. Unaffected by the heat, Kibii started to jump in place with great concentration.

"What are you doing?" she asked.

Barely out of breath, he said, "To be a *murani*, I have to jump higher than myself." Kibii leapt up, higher and higher with each leap.

"What does jumping have to do with being a warrior?"

Arap Maina's slow voice answered, "It strengthens the legs."

Beryl started to jump, but her heavy boots raised clouds of dust, and she certainly wasn't jumping higher than her head. "My boots are too heavy."

"A *murani* doesn't make excuses," said Arap Maina, speaking to the sky.

"Take the boots off," said Kibii.

"The chiggers will get me." Beryl had experienced the nasty insects too many times. They burrowed into your toes and left their eggs there to hatch. A sharp needle, cleansed in a hot flame, was the only way to get rid of them.

"Curl your toes," Kibii said between hops. Beryl looked closely. Sure enough, Kibii's toes were in a permanent crunch.

Beryl hesitated. Her boots were her main defense against all the sharp and venomous things in Africa.

"Never mind, Beru," said Arap Maina. "Kibii has to practice his skills to be a warrior. But there is no need for you to take risks." His voice was kind, but to Beryl, his words stung like salt on an open cut. She felt her spine straighten.

Beryl pulled off her boots, then her thick socks. Bending her knees, she pushed off. Without the heavy boots, she achieved more height than she expected. For a split second, she flew.

"Beryl Clutterbuck, what on earth are you doing?" Her father strode over, his forehead dotted with perspiration under his pith helmet.

"Jumping," she said, panting.

"Why?" he asked.

"To strengthen my leg muscles for riding," she improvised, glad that Arap Maina and Kibii did not speak enough English to give her away.

"Put your boots on. I want you looking respectable when the train arrives."

"The horses don't care," Beryl muttered, lacing up her boots.

The Captain glanced at his pocket watch. "Where is that train?"

Arap Maina's sharp eyes spotted it first through the haze. He pointed down the hill, his long arm following his finger. "There!"

The steel-gray train slowly rolled into the station and, with a great sigh, heaved to a halt, clouds of stream billowing from beneath the wheels. The crew began hauling barrels of water to cool the overheated engine. Passengers covered with thick dust disembarked from the rear car. Porters appeared from nowhere, lugging hens and goats and boxes of produce. They began to unload the manufactured goods, postal packages, and red four-gallon cans of paraffin fuel, everything essential to colonists living far from civilization.

The Captain's attention was on the livestock car. The heavy door slid open and a stable lad pushed a metal ramp to the ground. After a moment of anticipation, the lad led a nervous bay stallion to the waiting Clutterbucks.

"His name is Camiscan," Captain Clutterbuck murmured to Beryl, his eyes riveted on the thoroughbred's reddish-gold coat. The horse was a mass of muscle, but lean, built for speed and stamina. "Out of Spearmint, and his dam is from a top Australian mare. Beryl, this stallion will establish me as the top breeder in Africa." A white star on the horse's forehead promised greatness to come.

Camiscan lifted his nose high and sniffed the highland air. He tossed his head, and his glossy skin quivered with questions. Beryl glanced at Kibii and Arap Maina. Kibii's mouth hung open and Arap Maina's eyes were admiring. Before they came to Green Hills farm, they had never seen a thoroughbred, only poor excuses for horses—donkeys crossed with zebras. But even the Captain's other horses couldn't hold a candle to Camiscan.

The wind shifted, bringing a musky smell from the next valley.

"Lion," said Arap Maina.

Every farmer knew the smell, but to the stallion it was new and dangerous. Camiscan neighed loudly, almost a scream, and jerked his head. Without warning, the stallion reared up, tearing the rope from the lad's hands. The boy dropped to the ground and rolled into a ball, whimpering with fear.

The nervous stallion screamed again. He wheeled right, then left, looking for a way out. He charged at Arap Maina, who held his ground until the last moment and then melted to one side. Camiscan galloped away from the noisy train and the strange smells.

Captain Clutterbuck started after the runaway. "Must I do everything myself?"

Beryl was faster than her father, and nearer. She leapt toward the lead that trailed behind the galloping horse. She landed on her belly, but her fingers closed on the thick rope.

"Capital, Beryl! You've got him!" her father shouted.

The road was hardly more than a dirt path. Her body bounced in every rut and against every stone. Beryl pulled herself up the rope. Her weight wasn't enough to stop Camiscan's flight, but he slowed a little, as though he were dragging a sack of oats.

"Daddy!"

"Don't let go, Beryl. He's worth the farm!" Beryl's father ran to catch up, but he wasn't fast enough. It was up to her. She knew horses follow their heads, so she clung for dear life, pulling Camiscan's head to the right, back toward the train. Finally, he turned, allowing the Captain to close the gap and catch his bridle.

"Whoa, boy, whoa," the Captain said. Beryl felt an enormous wave of relief; no one in the colony could soothe a horse like he could.

Stroking the stallion's withers, the Captain spoke in a quiet voice. "Beryl, you can let go. I've got him."

Her fingers were tightly clenched around the rope, and she found it hard to open her bruised hands. Arap Maina stepped forward and lifted her to her feet while Kibii pried open her fingers. Beryl's arms, legs, and face felt as though they had been scrubbed raw. Tears were welling up in her eyes until she saw the expressions on the faces of Arap Maina and Kibii. They were impressed. With her. The tears dried as though she had never been tempted to be so weak. Perhaps Arap Maina would let her hunt now.

The Captain calmed the horse, then examined his legs for damage. "He's faster than anything else in the colony. We would have had a job catching him if he had escaped. Well done, Beryl."

Beryl, propped up by Arap Maina's strong arm, felt as though she had wrestled a lion.

Glancing over his shoulder, the Captain said, "A beauty, don't you think, darling?"

"Yes, Daddy, he's gorgeous!" said Beryl.

"Beautiful indeed," said a woman whose arrival Beryl had not noticed. "But the child badly needs a bath and some bandaging. And that hair! I think there might actually be a bird's nest in there."

Beryl whirled around. A young woman stood there, sweltering in a long-sleeved white blouse and a heavy khaki skirt. Her head was encased in a double felt terai hat, to protect her complexion. Her hat and face were coated with a layer of red dust that made her violet eyes stand out like jewels. Her wide smile displayed perfect little white teeth.

The Captain chuckled in a way Beryl had never heard him laugh before. "I meant the horse."

"He's very nice, but my responsibility is this young . . . lady. I assume that she's a lady under all that dirt." Her voice was pure British, like cut glass. Beryl was reminded of her mother's voice, one of the few memories of her Beryl still had.

Resisting the urge to rub the dirt off her face, Beryl turned to her father. "Who's she?"

"Manners, Beryl. This is Mrs. Orchardson. She's come to take care of us."

Beryl took an involuntary step back.

"Call me Emma. I'm sure we're going to be great friends," Mrs. Orchardson said brightly. "I've heard so much about you."

Beryl stared at her, gritting her teeth. Finally she said, "Daddy never mentioned you. Not once."

Emma gave the Captain a hard look, and her smile grew tighter. "Then you must not know that I've brought my son, Arthur, too. He's just a year or two younger than you." She gestured gracefully to a slight boy just behind her. He had dark hair and pale skin. He was coughing.

"Is he sick?" Beryl had never been ill a day in her life.

"Asthma. That's why we've come to the highlands." She raised her voice a bit. "My husband and I hope the alpine air will be good for him." Beryl glanced around. The other settlers, all men, were gathering around, admiring the Captain's new housekeeper. Beryl had vague memories of men admiring her mother, too.

"Clutt," Emma said, "you said you were in the highlands, but I didn't expect it to be so remote."

He grinned sheepishly. "You should have seen it before the railroad was finished."

She coughed. "I'm not sure I would call it finished."

"A miracle of British ingenuity and perseverance," the Captain insisted.

"We had to get out and walk!" she retorted.

Arthur piped up, "The conductor said there was a lion outside where we stopped, but Mama said that was nonsense." His voice was thin, and it was hard to hear him over all the noise at the station.

"A horrid little man," Emma said. "Scaring little boys like that!"

Beryl interrupted, "If you have a husband, where is he?" Maybe this Mrs. Orchardson's visit would be short.

Emma's nostrils flared a little as if she scented a threat, but she answered politely. "He's an anthropologist, out in the bush for months at a time. I need a good challenge to keep me busy, and your father asked me to help out here . . ." Her voice trailed off. Her eyes went to Arap Maina's hand on Beryl's arm. "Clutt, should you permit this black man to touch Beryl?"

"This is Arap Maina, Emma," the Captain said. "He helps to run the farm and takes care of Beryl."

"He looks too menacing to be a nanny," Emma said. Her little laugh invited everyone except Arap Maina and Beryl to join in.

"Arap Maina is a warrior, not a nanny," Beryl protested. "Not that I need one, anyway. We are doing just fine on our own, right, Daddy?"

The Captain refused to meet her eyes. "Beryl, you will treat our guests properly and make them feel at home." A porter touched his arm and spoke quickly. The Captain's face fell. "Emma—I mean, Mrs. Orchardson, how much luggage did you bring?"

She raised her finely shaped eyebrows. "You told me that the conditions were primitive, so I brought everything! We'll soon make Green Hills farm a proper home." She frowned at Beryl. "Happily, I brought some extra hats for Beryl. What have you let her do to her complexion? She looks like a field hand!"

The Captain ran his finger inside his collar, as though it had gotten tighter. "I'm going to have to send the big wagon down from the farm to bring it all back. Come and select what you need for today." He handed Beryl the lead for Camiscan. "Take the horse home. Arap Maina will go with you. After I sort out the luggage, I'll take Emma and Arthur home in the mule cart."

Without giving Beryl a chance to complain, he held out a hand to Emma and they followed the porter to the baggage car. Arthur trailed behind them, coughing pitifully.

Beryl's eyes were fixed on the back of Emma's felt hat. Emma stopped, murmuring something to the Captain. Glancing back at Beryl, he kept walking. Emma came back, hopping a little as though her pointy-up boots hurt her feet. Beryl's aching hands clenched into fists, and Camiscan shifted nervously beside her.

"Beryl," Emma began. "I'm sorry we started off on the wrong foot, but I'm here to help. You must have missed a woman's touch about the house."

The house. Now she understood why her father had built a proper house with doors and windows and wooden floors. Mama left because she had to live in a mud hut. No doubt Daddy had learned his lesson. This Emma person would bolt even faster than Mama had. How long had he planned this?

"My mother didn't last out here. Neither will you."

Emma's cheeks pinked. "I'm here to stay."

"Not if I have anything to say about it." Beryl clucked to Camiscan. With a nervous skitter, the stallion permitted her to lead him away.

"Beryl, we can be friends or we can be enemies," Emma called to her. "Which is it going to be?"

"*Kita!*" Beryl answered in Swahili, smiling to see Emma's bewildered look. It would indeed be war.

My maps and compass are packed. I won't bring a change of clothing—I can't afford the weight. How liberating to cross the ocean with only the shirt on my back! It's a grand adventure, and I'll leave England's shores with no regrets.

Well, perhaps one. I wish I could say good-bye to Tom. He's off on a record-breaking flight of his own. If I make it across the Atlantic, it's because of his patient training. His skills are in my hands and in my head.

I know he won't mind. Friends from Africa are like that—they appear and disappear from your life. You don't understand that you're lonely until you meet them. And when they're gone, you carry on.

But it would be nice to hear his voice before I go. I'll just have to settle for a transatlantic phone call the day after tomorrow. He'll drawl, "What's all the fuss about? I knew you could do it, Beryl."

CHAPTER FIVE

BERYL HOOKED ONE ANKLE AROUND KIBII'S LEG AND SWEPT HIM off his feet. In an instant, she had her heel on his chest. She clasped her hands over her head and chanted, "I won! I won!" It was the first time she had beaten Kibii at wrestling.

"You were lucky," Kibii said. "I tripped over a branch."

"A warrior doesn't make excuses," Beryl said, mimicking Arap Maina's deep voice.

"A true warrior has no need to brag," he answered back.

"I still won."

Kibii scowled and looked around for any new subject. His eyes lit on the house. "Cluttabucki's new house is very handsome," he said.

Beryl shrugged.

Visitors always marveled at how quickly a new hut went up in British East Africa: When guests arrived, the Captain ordered his men to throw together a hut made of mud and sticks. Everyone, even children, had a private hut. But the house was different. It was bigger, for one thing. And instead of a mud floor, he had used wide wooden planks from his new mill in the valley. And the Captain had built a real fireplace. Every night, the smell of burning cedar drifted through the compound. Beryl couldn't help thinking that if her father had built this house earlier, Mama might have stayed. Instead, it was Emma and Arthur who had made themselves at home with crate after crate of dishes, linens, and bric-a-brac.

"You still live in your old hut." Kibii had a way of making a flat statement a question.

"I won't live with that woman. She wants me to take baths!"

"Your new mother?"

Beryl whirled around and shoved Kibii's chest with her palm. "She's not my mother!" she growled.

Kibii took a step back. "Very well. She is your second mother, like Naipende is mine."

"She'll never be any sort of mother at all." Beryl's voice caught, as though she had tripped over a root. She cleared her throat and continued. "I do very well in my hut, thank you very much!"

Cautiously, Beryl skirted the wide front porch. There was no sign of Emma. The Captain had given in to Emma's demand for a household staff to help her "turn out" the house. Beryl couldn't go near the building without being caught in a cloud of dust from Emma's frenetic cleaning.

"I'll race you to my hut!" Beryl said, and took off. Kibii was close behind. They ran behind the cooking hut where all the meals for the family and the workers were prepared. They continued past the small building where laundry was done and flew around the corner to Beryl's hut, skidding crazily.

Kibii stumbled over a small pile of crates. Beryl caught her breath. The crates were hers, and they contained all of her prized belongings. A bit of tusk from the elephant that had got caught in the gully on the north side of the farm. The silver-backed hairbrush that had belonged to her mother. One of her father's racing trophies. Her father's medal for winning the mythology competition at school. Beryl snatched up the tarnished brush. She advanced on her hut, brandishing it like a weapon.

Emma bustled out of the doorway, her khaki skirt streaked with dust. Her hair was covered by a white linen handkerchief. She was busily directing a small crew of houseboys to bring the rest of Beryl's things outside.

Buller was sleeping in the sun, safely out of the way. When he saw Beryl, his tail thumped, raising a puff of dust, and then he covered his eyes with his front paws.

"Get the hell out of my house," Beryl shouted.

"I won't tolerate such language, Beryl." Emma frowned. "Where did you learn such words?"

"Daddy taught me," Beryl nodded sharply and placed her hands on her hips.

Emma sighed. "I'm cleaning, my dear. It seems to me that there is enough dust in your hut to fill the Sahara." Her dark hair was coming loose from her kerchief, and her pert nose was smudged with dirt.

"It's a mud hut," Beryl pointed out. "What do you expect?"

"Standards, my dear. That's why I am here: to keep us up to basic standards."

"Get out! My father . . ."

"Your father has asked me to keep house. Why he lets you stay here in squalor instead of being in a proper home, I cannot imagine. But if you insist, I'm going to make sure it's hygienic."

Beryl frowned. She had no idea what hygienic meant, but she didn't want her home to suffer from it.

Emma held up a string of colored beads. "What are these? I found them around your bed."

Kibii drew in a sharp breath.

"Kibii gave them to me," Beryl said. "They protect me at night."

Emma narrowed her eyes. "Protect you against what?"

"The devil." Beryl grinned to see the look of horror on Emma's face as she threw the beads to the ground. Kibii darted forward and grabbed the beads, tucking them inside his *shuka*.

"I'm going to have to talk to your father about this," Emma said. "The devil indeed!"

"My hut is my private place."

"You're ten years old; you don't have private places."

"I'm almost eleven!" Beryl cried. "I gave you the whole house— why can't you just leave me this little hut?"

"You ran away from your father's house like a wild thing; you did not give me the house. And I'm still not happy with you sleeping out here alone. All these natives . . ."

Emma glanced nervously at Kibii, who was listening intently. His English was getting better by the day, but he still had to concentrate to understand. "It's not safe. A young girl should sleep safely under her father's roof."

"Are you saying the Nandi are dangerous?" Beryl rolled her eyes. "Because that's just stupid. Arap Maina is teaching me to be a warrior. What can you teach me? Housecleaning?"

"Don't be foolish, Beryl. You're an English girl; you can't be a warrior."

"Better a warrior than a housemaid!"

Emma drew herself up. "I am not a maid. I run your father's house."

"You don't run *me*."

"If I did, you would be clean and polite, like Arthur."

Beryl made a face. She had barely seen Arthur outside the house since he arrived. "He's a namby-pamby mama's boy. He's afraid of everything."

Emma's fingers on the broom gripped so tightly that the blood drained out of them. "He's delicate."

"If he came into the forest with me, he wouldn't stay delicate for long."

"With *you*!" All the scorn and disbelief in the world fit into Emma's single syllable. "I'd never expose Arthur to such a risk."

"Then he'll always be a namby-pamby."

Emma made a frustrated sound and turned back to her cleaning. She called to a houseboy: "Bring out the bed. I'm sure it's filthy under there, too."

"I wouldn't do that if I were you," Beryl warned.

The houseboy called out something from inside the hut. Emma crinkled her nose, trying to make out the words. "What did he say, Beryl?"

"He wants to show you what's under my bed," Beryl said, her lips twitching.

Kibii started to speak, but Beryl silenced him with a hand gesture behind her back.

Emma, brushing her hair from her damp forehead, strode back into the hut.

Beryl moved closer to the door to listen. There was a brief exchange between Emma and the houseboy. A dragging of the bed. Then a muffled scream. Beryl stepped back just in time. Emma burst from the door, shrieking in terror. Something like a thick rug covered her shoulders.

"Get it off me!" The rug moved and became a long arm. Its eerily human hand pulled the handkerchief off Emma's head. She screamed again. "Help me! Clutt! Help!"

With a hoot and thump of his paw against his chest, the hairy rug let go of Emma's back and stretched an arm to the sill of the door. With one motion, the baboon swung himself off Emma and onto the roof of Beryl's hut. In an instant he was gone, leaving echoes of his raucous laughter behind.

Emma sank to the ground, weeping, her face buried in her skirt. The houseboys melted away with broad smiles on their faces. Beryl and Kibii were doubled over with laughter. Arap Maina, alerted by the noise, came running.

He barked a short word of inquiry to Kibii, who quickly answered back: "*Nyani*."

"Emma, it was only Daddy's pet baboon, Simi," Beryl said. "Stop crying." She might have explained that Simi slept under her bed most days to escape the heat of the afternoon, but why borrow trouble?

Arap Maina's expression was more grave than usual. He knelt down, his braids swinging and clicking, and offered his hand to Emma.

Staring wildly, Emma cried, "Don't touch me!" She pushed herself off the ground and stumbled to her feet. Half-running, she weaved uncertainly back to the main house.

"Beru, you must show more respect to your elders." Arap Maina's voice was stern.

"I warned her not to disturb my bed," Beryl said virtuously.

"She did," confirmed Kibii.

"It was not worthy, Beru," Arap Maina said. "I teach the *totos* to be kind to those who are afraid. And your new mother is very afraid."

"She's not my mother!" Beryl shouted.

Arap Maina stared at her with his quiet eyes. She stared back defiantly, but after a moment his silent authority won.

"I'm sorry, Arap Maina," she mumbled.

He inclined his head, braids dangling but dignified as always. "Kibii, come. We have much to prepare for tonight."

"What's happening tonight?" Beryl asked eagerly.

"We kill the leopard," Kibii said.

Emma was forgotten. "Arap Maina, I want to help!" Beryl said quickly.

Arap Maina considered. "You may select the goat we will use for the trap," he offered.

"I know a nasty billy goat." Beryl smiled wickedly. "Where do I bring him?"

"The water tank in the north field. It is far enough from the horses." Arap Maina smoothed his rows of wire necklaces. "Bring the goat. Then you must go back to your hut."

"But that's not fair. I want to help."

She heard Kibii mutter, "When will she learn that girls don't hunt?"

"Arap Maina, you said I was brave," Beryl said.

"Beru, this leopard is dangerous." Arap Maina's face was set. "I will hear no more about it." He walked away, his feet barely seeming to touch the ground.

"I told you, this is men's work!" Kibii abandoned her to run after his father.

Buller came over to nuzzle Beryl's hand with his wet nose. She stood still, watching Arap Maina's back. "Buller, I'm going to hunt . . . no matter what."

A nosy reporter just asked me why I'm doing it. Why am I flying to America by myself? Why take the risk? I give him my usual answer about opening new commercial routes to America, but the truth is far simpler. I never could resist a dare.

It began only a few months ago. There had been lobster, champagne, and a jazz band so noisy you couldn't hear your dinner partner. Lord J. C. Carberry, a thoroughly unpleasant man but a generous host, leaned across the table, his black eyes glittering in their sunken sockets.

"Beryl," he said loudly, capturing everyone's attention. "What do you think of this woman Earhart? She's a snappy dresser."

"What does it matter what Amelia Earhart wears? She's a smashing pilot," I said. What was the old fox up to?

"She crossed the Atlantic solo. Got a lot of publicity."

"Well deserved," I answered.

He glanced around the table. "She took the easy route, west to east. Do you care to try it the hard way?"

England to New York. East to west. Flying in the dark over the stormy North Atlantic. The winds against me. Chasing the morning.

After a bare moment, "I would . . . if I had a plane."

"It's a deal!" J. C. cried. "I provide the plane and you do the flying." He called for another bottle of champagne and we toasted my flight. Everyone laughed, clinked glasses, and drifted off to dance. Just as though there weren't pilots crashing every day to their deaths in the deserts, in the forests, into the freezing water.

Why did I say yes? Everyone was setting records in those days. Tom set one just the other day, flying from London to Melbourne in only 71 hours. It's my turn.

CHAPTER SIX

BY TWILIGHT, BERYL WAS TIRED OF WAITING. SHE'D DELIVERED the goat and left Arap Maina and Kibii to their task. But no sooner had the sun fully set than she was creeping toward the water tower. She wore a dark shirt and her filthiest trousers, to blend into the night. After a moment's consideration, she kept her shell bracelet on her wrist.

As she got closer, she could see Kibii crouched underneath a rusty water tank. Beyond him, lit by the rising moon, was a clearing where the miserable goat was tethered. Careful not to step on anything that would make a noise, Beryl moved forward.

Suddenly, her body was lifted from behind and she couldn't breathe. Arap Maina had pulled her up by the back of her shirt. She swung from his grip, like a cub in a lioness's mouth.

"Arap Maina," she cried. "How did you know I was coming?"

"Beru, you are louder than your goat and your yellow hair is easy to see in the dark," he scolded. "You must go home."

"Please let me stay," Beryl begged.

He shook his head. "Your father . . ." he began.

"Wants his livestock to be safe."

"He also wants his daughter to be safe."

"He asked you to teach me," Beryl reminded him. "And I want to learn, so I can help my father."

Arap Maina looked up at the sky as if to find inspiration from the bats and owls flying overhead.

"Please," Beryl said again. "At least let me watch."

"If I take you back to your hut, I might miss the leopard, and all our work will be undone." With a sigh, he put her down. "Kibii, come here."

"Father?" came Kibii's low voice. He emerged from the bushes, his steps silent. Then he saw Beryl and his tone became accusatory. "What is she doing here?"

"Take Beru to the top of the water tank. Stay with her and keep her safe."

"But we were to hunt together!" Kibii protested.

"I don't need protecting!" Beryl exclaimed at the same instant.

Arap Maina pointed. They climbed up the tank's ladder.

"I'm sorry, Kibii," she said as they lay on their stomachs. He didn't answer.

The moon continued its long arc into the sky. The surface of the water tank was hard and bumpy against Beryl's stomach. Nothing moved below. The goat bleated, as if inviting a leopard to kill him.

"Kibii," she whispered. "I thought hunting would be more interesting."

"This is not hunting, it is minding a girl-child who does not know her place," he snarled. "Now, be quiet. If you can."

"Of course I can!"

"Ssshh!"

The moon climbed higher in the sky. Beryl sighed and fingered the shell on her bracelet. She shifted on the rusty metal and heard water sloshing in the tank.

"Ssshh!" Kibii hissed.

The water reminded her of an unpleasant pressure on her bladder. The bright light of Venus had almost faded into nothing. Trying to distract herself, she counted the stars appearing, taking special note of each constellation as it formed.

"Look, there's Cetus. That's the whale. My father taught me all about the constellations. I've never seen a whale. . . . I don't even remember seeing the ocean."

Beryl heard grinding. She looked over and thought it might be Kibii gritting his teeth.

"Answer me, Kibii. I'm bored."

A hushing sound was the only answer. Beryl sighed. She had hoped for so much from the leopard hunt, but instead she was stuck on this tank, out of harm's way.

Lips clamped shut, she inched to the edge to look straight down. The tethered goat was still crying. She felt a moment's sympathy, but then she remembered that it always butted her with its bonehard horns, and how it had nipped Arthur just yesterday.

Beryl looked around. The forest was as dark and empty as it had been all evening. Unable to ignore her bladder any longer, she rolled over and clambered down from the tank.

"Beru, come back," Kibii whispered.

"I can't wait."

She landed hard, turning her ankle on a branch. "Ow," she began to say, when a hand came out of the darkness and clamped down on her mouth.

Arap Maina's silhouette against the moon towered over her. She could not see his face but his spicy smell was unmistakable. The moonlight glinted off his oiled chest. Beryl realized it was the first time she had ever seen him without his necklaces. "Beru, I told you to wait above," he whispered, but Beryl could hear his disapproval. "You must learn to listen."

"It's very uncomfortable up there, Arap Maina," she said. "And I have to relieve myself." She blushed a little.

She thought she saw a quick smile pass across his face. Then it was gone. "Do what you need to do, but do it quickly," he said.

A few moments later, feeling much better, Beryl returned. "Any sign of the leopard?" she asked Arap Maina.

"The leopard will not come if you are talking."

Beryl tugged on the tuft of her untidy braid. "But it's been hours, and nothing has happened."

"We may have to wait another night. A *murani* does not mind waiting." He paused. "And a *murani* is always quiet."

She could make out Kibii's motionless outline on the water tank. He hadn't moved a muscle.

"I'll do better," she promised.

Arap Maina made an exasperated noise. "Silence! Or perhaps you would prefer to join the women in the village again?"

"No, thank you," Beryl said loudly.

"Hush!" Kibii and Arap Maina burst out together.

She silently climbed back to her perch on the tank.

The hours passed. Each time Beryl began to fall asleep, she would jerk herself awake. She was drifting off again when she heard Arap Maina's low whistle. She peeked down to see a barely visible spotted shadow where the forest began.

Baa-aah. The goat ran frantically in the narrow circle around his tether, bleating with terror. Beryl felt a pang for the little animal. But then she thought of Buller.

The leopard, its stomach brushing the ground, crept closer to the goat. Beryl couldn't tear her eyes away. This was the animal who had walked, bold as brass, into her own hut and taken her dog. Then she had been afraid, huddled on her bed. But now she was with warriors. Though he didn't know it yet, the predator had become the prey.

The moon was high now. Beryl could see Arap Maina holding his spear in front of him, moving toward the tethered goat as stealthily as the leopard.

The leopard sank back on its haunches and leapt to the goat's back. Beryl winced at the cracking of the goat's backbone. The leopard rolled off and grabbed the goat's throat between its jaws and ripped. Beryl shuddered, thinking of Buller's barely healed wounds. Backing away from the tank's edge, she was suddenly content to be safely out of the way.

Arap Maina appeared. With one thrust, he put his spear through the leopard's neck. A high-pitched whine and the leopard was dead.

Kibii scrambled down from the top of the water tank. Beryl slowly followed. She stared down at the goat's carcass. Vomit rose into her throat at the metallic smell of fresh blood. She had seen animals slaughtered before for meat and skin, but she had never seen one ripped apart by sharp teeth.

Now the leopard seemed small and not fierce at all. Its coat was covered with barely healed scars.

Arap Maina's eyes were luminous in the night, and he shivered as though he were cold.

"Father," Kibii said. "I saw how you waited until he was distracted by his dinner. The fresh blood of the goat filled his nose, so he could not scent you."

Beryl interrupted, eager to show how much she, too, had observed. "He didn't hear you coming because he was making so much noise with his eating."

Arap Maina nodded his approval, still breathing hard through his nose. He pulled his spear from the leopard's body and wiped it clean on the grass.

"You speared the heart," Beryl said.

"This leopard is not afraid of men. The heart was the safest way to kill it with one blow."

Kibii's eyes were wide, memorizing everything.

"But you were too late to save the goat," Beryl said. She averted her eyes from the bloody mess of the goat's entrails.

Kibii snorted, but Arap Maina simply shook his head. "The goat was dead as soon as we used him for bait."

Beryl's father always said it didn't do to get sentimental about animals. Except Buller, of course.

As though he could read her thoughts, Arap Maina pointed to the teeth marks on the leopard's skull. "This is certainly the same leopard who attacked the dog."

"Buller did that?" Beryl asked. Her heart swelled with pride; Buller might have lost the fight, but he had done a lot of damage.

Arap Maina nodded. "He is a warrior, your dog."

"I saved Buller," said Kibii, thumping his chest.

Beryl insisted, "You would never have looked for him if I hadn't gone out into the forest."

"You would never have found him without me," Kibii answered. "And it is my medicine that heals him."

"He's a British dog," Beryl said in a voice to end the argument.

"None of our dogs would fight a leopard," Kibii admitted.

"Hush, *totos*," Arap Maina said, but he was smiling.

"Next time, I will fight with you," Beryl said.

Kibii hooted, "You are a girl—you won't ever fight."

Beryl shoved him. "I will too. Your father said I can train as a *murani*."

Arap Maina held up a hand, and both children instantly stopped speaking. "I permitted you to watch this night, but only the boys of the tribe hunt. Never the girls."

Beryl nudged the dead leopard with her foot. Its sightless eyes stared up at her.

"Arap Maina, I can be as brave as any boy." Deliberately, she untied her new bracelet and handed it back to him. "I'll only be one of the tribe if I can be a *murani*."

Kibii laughed so hard, he had to sit down. But Arap Maina was thoughtful. He glanced toward her father's house, then at the bracelet in his hand.

"We shall see," he said. "But first you must learn discipline. And obedience."

Beryl grimaced. She was going to have to wait a long time.

The Daily Express **Correspondent:** Mrs. Markham, we have some more questions for you.

Markham: Haven't you already had your pound of flesh? Why do you keep following me around?

Correspondent: Our readers are clamoring to know.

Markham: That's what all you vultures say when you invade my privacy. (sigh) Go ahead.

Correspondent: What provisions will you bring for the big flight?

Markham: Some roast chicken. Dried fruit and nuts. Five flasks of coffee. I'll need to stay awake, you know.

Correspondent: And how do you . . . how should I ask this? After all, there's no W.C. at two thousand feet!

Markham: Can you possibly ask anything more personal? Even in the solitude of the cockpit, I can't get away from you.

Correspondent: Mrs. Markham?

Markham: Very well. I've trained since I was a child to master my body's needs. Put that in your pipe and smoke it!

CHAPTER SEVEN

ARAP MAINA SOUNDED THE GONG EVERY MORNING TO CALL THE men to work. Beryl waited by the door to her hut, her feet already laced into her boots, her linen shirt tucked into her khaki trousers.

Dong. Dong.

That was the signal. Beryl sprinted to the main house. She and Kibii raced to the porch each morning, she from her hut and he from below the stables. They were scrupulous about the rules: neither could start before the gong, and the distance was precisely measured in paces. On this day, both sets of feet, booted and barefoot, hit the steps of the wooden porch at precisely the same time.

"I win!" Kibii crowed. His scarlet *shuka* was fastened securely around his waist, and his dark skin glistened with a faint sheen of perspiration.

"I won!" Beryl shouted.

"You are fast, but you are still only a girl."

With that, Beryl launched herself at Kibii's stomach, determined to take him down. But Kibii had taught her that move and he slipped easily out of her way. As she barreled past him, he grabbed her arm and twisted it behind her back. With his other hand, he grabbed a hank of her long hair.

"Ow!" Beryl cried, glaring over her shoulder.

"You see," he said triumphantly. "A boy would never cry out!"

"That's not fair," Beryl said, wincing as she tried to free herself. "You don't have hair."

"You choose to give me that advantage," he crowed. "Admit that I won!"

"No!"

"Are you quarreling hyenas, or are you children?" came the quiet, amused voice of Arap Maina.

Instantly, Kibii let go of Beryl's arm and hair. Beryl smoothed her tangles behind her ears. Arap Maina examined them both. A shadow of disapproval crossed his face.

"Beru," he said, "you must do something about your hair."

"Not you too!" Beryl complained.

"Kibii shaves his head so that bugs will not find a home. You invite insects to live in your hair."

Kibii nodded in solemn agreement. His bald skull was indisputably bug-free.

Beryl scratched her scalp, which suddenly itched everywhere.

The door to the main house opened and her father appeared, immaculately dressed in polished boots, jodhpurs, and a neat white shirt. He carried a riding crop in his hand.

"Good morning," he said to them all. Shielding his eyes against the rising sun, he watched the workers arrive with satisfaction. A few months ago there had been two dozen men; now there were more than a hundred, and his cleared land stretched for a hundred acres. He was defeating the forest, transforming its felled trees into planks of wood to build houses for British settlers and provide firewood for the train. Beryl loved how her father stood with his weight settled back on his heels, proudly surveying his kingdom.

The moment was ruined when Arthur came out to the porch. He was wheezing, even in the cool air of morning. Beryl noted bitterly that he was dressed like a miniature version of her father. The Captain's hand rested casually on Arthur's shoulder. Beryl felt her heart skip a beat.

"What's he doing here?" she asked.

"I'm going to teach him to ride," the Captain replied, his attention still on the workers streaming in to the stables and the mills.

"He's a crybaby," Beryl said. "And he's only eight."

"I'm nine," Arthur interrupted.

"And you're only ten," her father said.

"I'm eleven now, Daddy."

"The Baron was foaled the same year you were born, and he's in his tenth season."

"I'm not a horse, Daddy. I have birthdays."

"Did I miss your birthday?" he asked, momentarily distracted from the farm.

Beryl shrugged. The calendar meant little to her.

"And I'm not a crybaby," Arthur chirped.

"You are so!"

"Beryl, leave him alone." The Captain paused, then said, "The stable is growing; I'm going to need more lads. Might as well use what we have." He switched to Swahili. "Kibii, you'll be learning to ride, too."

"A horse?" Kibii asked, his voice a pale echo of his usual confident tone.

Beryl forgot her nervousness to lord over Kibii. "Come on—you said it didn't look hard. I dare you!" She grinned at her father, who smiled back. He was always telling her stories about the dares he and his fellow cavalry officers had performed in his military days.

Kibii narrowed his eyes at Beryl. "Your British horses do not frighten me. I accept your dare."

"We'll need some boots—even Kibii can't ride barefoot." The Captain turned to Beryl. "We're schooling Camiscan today. He's already saddle-broken, but he has to be in top condition. The racing season starts in three months."

Beryl smiled. Watching her father train the great stallion would be a treat.

"And Beryl, you will be riding him."

"Me?" she squeaked.

"I'll be working with you, but you'll be on his back. He likes you. We'll need every advantage with that horse." He glanced down at her and grinned, a challenge in his eyes. "Do you think you can do it?"

Kibii had a wicked grin on his face as he worked out what the Captain was daring Beryl to do.

She swallowed hard on her fear and nodded. "I won't let you down, Daddy." But her mind's eye was filled with Camiscan's bulk and the wild tossing of his massive head.

Arap Maina waited patiently for his assignment. The Captain spoke in Swahili. "I need you supervising at the mill. The men are getting careless. Yesterday one lad nearly crushed his hand in the grindstone." Arap Maina nodded and moved off.

Thirty minutes later in the paddock, Beryl regretted her rash words. Camiscan seemed intent on proving his superiority to mere humans, lowering his neck and charging anyone who came near. Only when the Captain held the horse's head still was Beryl able to throw a lightweight saddle across his back. The moment the stirrups touched his sides, Camiscan began snapping with bared teeth.

"Daddy, he doesn't like the stirrups," Beryl said, proud that her voice was steady.

"He's been ridden before. He's just trying to show you he's in charge. He can't race without stirrups, but can you mount without them for now?"

Beryl reached up and caught hold of the pommel and vaulted onto Camiscan's back. The stallion neighed nervously, but the Captain held the horse's head steady. Beryl perched on his back, seventeen hands high. Kibii and Arthur pressed themselves into a corner and stared up at Beryl, wide-eyed.

"Move out." The Captain watched closely, but Camiscan behaved himself, responding to Beryl's signals. "All right. Walk him around the paddock while I get the boys sorted out. Don't do anything else until I'm with you."

Beryl didn't spare the boys a thought as they began their lesson on two small ponies. She was too busy establishing a relationship with the giant horse.

"Good boy," she said. "You're a beauty. Not another horse in Africa can touch you." Camiscan snorted and pranced sideways, but gradually began to tolerate her on his back. Each turn around the paddock, Beryl grew more confident. She only wished her father would notice how well she was doing.

Instead of admiring Beryl's light touch with Camiscan, the Captain was occupied teaching Arthur and Kibii the basics of posture and where to put their feet. After he set the boys to plodding around the track, he came back to her and they put Camiscan through his paces. Beryl was perfectly content until she spied a figure marching down from the house.

"That Woman is coming."

"Don't call her that," the Captain said, not taking his eyes off Camiscan's stride. "Her name is Emma."

Emma marched with a determined look. She was dressed in a bright white blouse and an impeccable khaki skirt. By afternoon, her ensemble would be covered by the dust that swirled around the farm and her dustcloth. And then she would change into an evening gown for dinner. Beryl shook her head, disgusted by all that wasted effort.

"What does she want now?" the Captain muttered. "She chased me out of my own study with that damned dust rag."

"Clutt, when are you coming to breakfast?" Emma called as she approached the fence. Her arms were tightly crossed across her chest. "It's been ready for half an hour." The color rose in her cheeks and she began breathing quickly. "Oh, my goodness! You put Arthur on a horse?"

"Of course; he lives on a horse farm."

"He's too delicate—"

Beryl and Camiscan snorted, united in their scorn of Emma.

"I'll toughen him up," the Captain said.

For the first time, Emma noticed who was riding Camiscan. "Beryl's on that terrible stallion?"

Now it was the Captain who shot her a scornful look. "That horse is the future of this farm."

"He's too dangerous for a little girl. Why aren't you riding him?"

The Captain scowled. "Emma, I can't do everything around here. Camiscan needs exercising every day. Beryl is my best rider. Don't worry; Arthur and Kibii will soon be good riders, too."

"You're teaching them together?" Emma glanced over at Kibii, whose long legs practically dragged on the ground from the back of his little pony. His expression was bored, even embarrassed, while Arthur looked petrified, clutching the reins as though his life depended on it.

"What's wrong with Kibii?" Beryl demanded, bringing Camiscan to a stop in front of Emma.

"Nothing, not a thing," Emma stammered, stepping behind the Captain to be as far from Camiscan as possible. "But Kibii and Beryl are strong, and Arthur is . . ."

"*Del*-i-cate." Kibii carefully pronounced the syllables of the strange word he heard so often.

The Captain and Beryl burst out laughing.

Wringing her dustcloth between her hands, Emma's jaw tightened. Her eyes were furious. "It's all very well for the two of you to cackle like witches. But Clutt, you should have consulted me before you put Arthur on a horse."

"It's not a horse, it's a measly little pony," Beryl called from her perch high on Camiscan's back.

"Some people have the sense to be afraid of large animals that could kill them," Emma said, glaring at Beryl.

"Enough, Beryl," the Captain snapped. "Emma, you're upsetting Camiscan." He slapped his riding crop against his leg. "Beryl, Emma and I have to talk. Take him around at a half gallop."

As the Captain and Emma argued at the fence, Beryl took a deep breath, clucked for Camiscan to run, and pressed her heels to his flank. The stallion nearly unseated her with a half leap and a burst of untamed speed. She burst out laughing from exhilaration mixed with a little bit of terror. She passed Kibii and Arthur as if they were standing still. The look on Kibii's face was pure envy. Beryl felt as if she could soar off into the sky above the valley.

The third time she rounded past the boys, Arthur's pony veered into her path. As though they were all moving extraordinarily slowly, Beryl saw Arthur turn his head to face her, his mouth hanging open in a silent scream. She could see the whites of the pony's eyes as he saw Camiscan charging up on his flank. The pony reared and Arthur slid to the ground like a sack of maize.

Beryl pulled the reins toward the inside of the paddock, dragging Camiscan's head with all the power in her arms. Furious at such disrespect, the stallion bucked and kicked, doing everything he could to dislodge his rider.

"Arthur!" Emma screamed. She began to scramble through the fence, catching her skirt on a nail.

"Beryl, pull up!" the Captain shouted. "Pull up!"

Camiscan arched his back and kicked out with his rear legs at the same time. Beryl was thrown back and she bit her lip. She tried every trick she knew to keep her seat, but the stallion's bucking was too violent. She was losing.

"Rein him in, Beryl!"

"I'm trying, Daddy," she cried. "He's too strong."

Arthur lay ominously still on the ground. Emma gathered him in her arms, screaming for the Captain. "Clutt, help him!"

"Beryl, hold on," the Captain said. He tore his eyes from Camiscan and Beryl and moved quickly to Emma's side to check on Arthur.

As though he had been showing off for Captain Clutterbuck, Camiscan came to a sudden halt. Beryl heaved a sigh of relief and leaned forward to pat the stallion's long neck.

"Bad boy. Bad, bad boy," she whispered. Holding the reins in one hand, she wiped her forehead with the other. She glanced at Arthur, who was sitting up with a dazed look on his face.

That was Camiscan's chance. Before Beryl knew what had happened, the stallion's head twisted back toward her. His huge teeth grabbed her shoulder and dragged her off his back. She hung there, suspended between his great jaws, the pain in her shoulder making her head swim. Camiscan threw her in the air like a cat might torment a mouse. She fell to the ground with a thud, still gripping the reins.

"Beru!" Kibii shouted. "Cluttabucki, help her!"

The impact had knocked the breath out of Beryl. Her only reality was the throbbing in her shoulder and the jerking of her whole body as the stallion tossed his head at the other end of the reins. Camiscan neighed loudly, as though to say he was still the king.

From far away, Beryl heard her father snap at Emma to stop caterwauling and be useful. She felt his confident hands as he checked her wound. He pried the rein from her fingers and she heard the soft clopping of Camiscan's hooves moving away. Hours later—or perhaps it was only moments—her father, with surprising gentleness, was helping her sit up. Arthur, none the worse for wear, and Kibii stared down at her with something close to awe in their eyes.

"Beryl, talk to me," the Captain said. "Can you hear me?"

"Daddy," she croaked. She touched her shoulder. No blood, just a soreness that was bound to be black and blue by evening.

He smiled and lifted her to her feet. "You're all right?" he asked as he gave her a quick hug.

Beryl staggered for a moment until her natural balance won out over her wobbling legs. She nodded.

"Get back on, then." The Captain gestured to Camiscan, tied to the fence.

"Clutt, she can't!" Emma cried.

Kibii muttered something in Swahili, and Arthur looked green. Beryl's lip throbbed.

"All right," she said. "Tomorrow."

"Now." He was merciless. "You have to show him that he can't throw you and get away with it."

"I just have to catch my breath," she pleaded.

He waited, his gray eyes measuring her courage.

She beckoned him closer. "Daddy, I'm scared," she whispered, afraid to meet the disapproval in his face. To her surprise, his words were kind, almost gentle.

"Of course you are," he said. "I would be, too."

"Really?"

He nodded. "But that doesn't change what you have to do."

He made it sound impossibly simple, Beryl thought. But she had trusted him her whole life. She nodded.

"That's my girl."

She walked stiffly to Camiscan. Her father lifted the reins back over the stallion's head and cupped his hands to lift her into the saddle.

"Don't trust him for a minute," the Captain warned.

When Beryl clucked, Camiscan moved off with a stride as smooth as silk, a perfect gentleman. As she led the stallion through his paces, she could feel the admiring eyes of the Captain, Emma, and the boys on her. She sat even straighter, careful not to wince, no matter how her shoulder ached.

"She's got as good a seat on a horse as any man," the Captain said to Emma. "Her mother was the same."

Beryl glanced at Emma. Under the dirt and tears, Emma's face was grim.

"Boys, watch Beryl and learn," the Captain said. "She just showed you two important lessons. No matter what happens, don't let go of the reins. And never let a horse think he has the upper hand." He moved to the gate. "All right. Back to the stable." As Beryl steered Camiscan through the narrow gate, her father touched her knee. "Well done."

Beryl grinned all the way back to the stables, knowing that she would wear the bruises on her shoulder like a badge of honor.

I was a terrible student with my governess and then at school. I only paid attention to things that interested me, and those teachers didn't know anything that interested me.

My real teachers taught me how to survive and thrive in Africa. My father taught me to ride and to trust my instincts to stay on a horse. Arap Maina taught me discipline and how to handle a spear. And Tom Black taught me to fly. None of them were ever easy on me. They knew the only way to teach survival was for me to experience danger firsthand. I remember best those lessons that nearly killed me.

Once I was flying with Tom Black over the Great Rift Valley toward the Ngong Hills. My altimeter said we were eight thousand feet above sea level. I opened the throttle to climb. But the plane was sluggish; she had no more to give. We were doing eighty miles an hour, fast enough that I didn't want to discover what would happen if we didn't clear the hills. More stick, more throttle. The weight on the wings grew heavier. I was just a beginner and I was beginning to get a bit rattled, but not Tom. He sat in the cockpit, motionless and silent, carefree.

The wall of rock was rushing toward us before Tom took the controls. He banked sharply, dusting the trees and hills with blue exhaust. He put the nose of the Gipsy down until we were skimming the flat valley floor. Then he spiraled up until we were high above the hills and headed home.

"Now you know what a downdraft is," said Tom casually. "You get it near mountains, and in Africa it's common as rain. I could have warned you—but you shouldn't be robbed of your right to make mistakes."

Is there a better way to learn?

CHAPTER EIGHT

CAMISCAN'S HIDE TWITCHED UNDER BERYL'S HAND. SHE PRESSED her palm against his withers and spoke sternly. "Boy, I'm going to keep grooming you every morning and night. You just have to get used to it." Camiscan still preferred Beryl to anyone else, but she was careful not to turn her back on him.

"Beryl, I'm bored." Arthur's head popped up over the stall door. "Will you play with me?" Although his fair skin was peeling from the sun, his breathing problems had improved in the clear air of the highlands. Under Beryl's tutelage, he was becoming an expert on the dangers of Africa. Emma would faint if she knew how expert.

"I'm working, Little A. Go away."

His voice, already high-pitched, became a whine. "There's nothing to do here! I'm bored."

Camiscan was growing restless. She thought for a moment.

"Play with Simi," she suggested.

"The monkey who scared Mama?" Arthur asked doubtfully.

"He's a baboon!" Beryl corrected with scorn. "And he was just defending himself after she poked a broom in his face. His favorite toy is that red ball—he'll play catch for hours."

"Will you come with me?"

"I told you. I'm working." She turned back to Camiscan and brushed his long legs. "Simi's probably on the porch underneath that bench."

"All right." He trudged off, kicking the dirt.

Beryl smiled to herself and patted Camiscan. "Arthur had better watch out," she murmured to the stallion. "Or else he'll get a big clout across the head. Simi doesn't like to share."

Her hand was closing the latch of the stall to lock Camiscan in for the night when a shriek split the evening. Only Simi sounded like that: like a human screaming, but without words. Beryl took off at a run in the direction of the house.

"Help!" Arthur cried.

"I'm coming!" she called.

Another baboon shriek. She had never heard Simi so angry.

Beryl took the shallow steps with a leap and skidded to a stop on the porch. "Simi!" she shouted. "Get away from him!"

The baboon had trapped Arthur in the corner of the porch. His arms wrapped around his head, Arthur had made himself as small a target as possible. His face had a huge welt. The baboon had struck once already.

"Simi, get away from him!" Beryl repeated. She smacked her hand against her leg, as her father did when he gave Simi an order.

Simi bared his sharp teeth. With contempt in his eyes, he turned back to the little boy.

Beryl's eyes shot around the compound. Where was Daddy? Where was Arap Maina?

"Help me, Beryl!" Arthur screamed.

"Don't move, Arthur." She was trembling, but her voice was steady.

Simi turned back to Arthur, and with a long swipe of his claws raked down the boy's shoulder. The blood welled up on the skin, and he shrieked from the pain.

Beryl darted in to grab Simi's arm. The animal must have had eyes in the back of his head. With his other arm, he reached across, lifted her by her shirt's collar, and threw her hard against the railing. She lay on the porch floor, the rough cedar pressed into her skin. A cut on her cheek bled, mixing with the tears rolling down her face. Simi was too strong for her.

The baboon moved toward Arthur. "Beryl!" he cried. "Do something!"

Beryl pushed herself up. She wouldn't fail again. She had to save Arthur. Casting about for a weapon—any weapon—she cursed herself for leaving her knife in her hut. Her eyes lit on her father's *rungu*, propped against the front door. She grabbed the narrow end of the walking stick and swung it in a wide circle above her head. The heavy, knobby end connected hard with the side of Simi's head.

Thwap.

The baboon went down like one of her father's trees.

Holding her breath, Beryl gripped the *rungu* in front of her. The baboon lay still on his side. She exhaled when she saw the widening pool of blood under his skull.

Arthur whimpered. Beryl spared him a glance. "Are you all right?" she asked.

He looked up at her, his face streaked with blood and tears. "Is he dead?"

"I think so." She approached the body. The baboon's face was unusually peaceful. It was easy to forget the wild beast and remember the years he'd been the family pet, to smile at the memory of all the pranks Simi had played.

"I'm sorry, Simi." She bent down to stroke his fur.

Simi's eyes popped open and Beryl stumbled backward. He screamed from deep inside his throat. The baboon's lips curled back and he leapt at Beryl's face, claws extended.

Without thinking, she struck out again with the *rungu*. Simi tried to grab it for himself. Beryl held the stick in front of her, like Arap Maina held a spear. She rammed the stick into Simi's body, crushing his stomach against the wall. Simi wrapped his arms around his body and hunched over. He hid his face the way baboons did when another creature bested them.

Beryl watched with wary eyes, *rungu* at the ready. With a quickening of her breath, she knew what Arap Maina would do. She had to finish this, or Arthur would pay the price later.

Another swing, and Simi's skull shattered. Brains and blood showered the wall. Arthur's hair and back were covered with little bits of baboon. Simi fell to the ground with a thud.

A moment later, the *rungu* fell from her hand. She touched her throbbing cheek with her fingertips.

"Beryl?" Arthur's voice trembled. "Is it over?"

"Yes, he's dead." She was panting.

"You said that before."

"He's really dead now."

She extended a hand to help him up. Arthur clung to her waist and began sobbing.

"Why are you crying now?" she asked. "It's over, you ninny." She hesitated, then reached down and put her arm around him.

In the corner, she spied the forgotten red ball.

Moments later, the Captain and Emma came running. Emma's anxious eyes searched only for her son.

"Arthur, what happened? We heard screaming . . ." She pulled him away from Beryl's arms, moaning at the bloody cuts. She ran her fingers over his face and shoulders. She glared at the Captain and said, "What did she do to him?"

"Emma, why don't you just ask me?" Beryl said in a flat voice. "And I didn't *do* anything to him. I *saved* him."

Emma ignored her and began speaking with Arthur in a low, urgent voice.

The Captain's keen eyes were examining the porch. He caught his breath at the sight of Simi's body. Then his gaze traveled to Arthur's injuries, the *rungu* dripping with gore, and finally to the flecks of blood spattered on Beryl's face and clothes.

"You killed Simi," he accused.

"I'm sorry, Daddy. I had to," Beryl said, without looking at his face.

"Do you know how much he cost? And that was three years ago—I'll never be able to get another." His voice was cold and angry. It took all of Beryl's courage not to run away.

Rescue came from an unexpected quarter.

"Charles Clutterbuck! Are you mad? That creature . . ." For once, Emma was not pointing an accusing finger at Beryl. "That vile beast nearly killed Arthur, who was only trying to play with him. Beryl saved his life. So don't you dare talk about money!"

Beryl finally looked at her father, deliberately widening her eyes so he wouldn't think to ask why Arthur was playing with the baboon in the first place.

"Why did you use my *rungu*?" the Captain asked in a more measured tone.

"I didn't have my knife. Arap Maina says a warrior should never be without his knife. I won't make that mistake again."

"A knife wouldn't have helped. Baboons have such a reach, you need a long weapon."

Beryl reviewed every detail of the fight in her mind. She nodded.

"You're both impossible!" Emma gathered Arthur in her arms, looking fiercely at the Captain. "This would never have happened if the children were properly supervised. And I don't mean by that native!"

"Emma, don't start this again. Simi had the run of the farm; this could have happened anywhere."

"Very reassuring, Clutt. This time we have a dead ape, but . . ."

"Baboon!" the Captain and Beryl said at the same time.

"The children need to be protected."

The Captain stepped forward and put his hands on Emma's shoulders. "Calm down. Simi is dead. Beryl took care of Arthur. Everything is fine."

Emma glared at him. "You're deluding yourself. An eleven-year-old girl was the only thing between my son and . . ." She couldn't finish the sentence. "Nothing is fine." She burst into hysterical tears. "I hate it here."

Beryl put her hands over her ears. The Captain looked as though he wanted to do the same. "Emma, take Arthur into the house and clean him up. Then we'll talk." He reached out and touched her hand. "Please?"

She shook off his touch and led Arthur inside, slamming the door hard.

"Whew." The Captain wiped his hand across his brow. "I don't know that I can talk us out of this one."

"Don't try. Let them leave."

The Captain sighed. "Emma's doing a lot of good around here. She's made this place a proper British home. Besides, I thought you liked Arthur."

Beryl thought about it for a moment. She remembered how Arthur hadn't tattled on Beryl to his mother. She owed him. "He's all right, I suppose. It's not his fault he's 'delicate.'"

A grin flashed across her father's face, replaced by a grim expression. Grunting a little, he bent down and lifted Simi's limp body. "Get cleaned up and have Emma look at that cut. I'll take this into the forest. The hyenas will take care of it."

After he left, Beryl sank down on the porch steps and breathed deeply. This time she had not cowered on her bed while an innocent victim was hurt. She had not stayed out of harm's way while someone else fought the battle for her. She had met the enemy and won. She couldn't wait to tell Kibii.

After two thousand flying hours in my log, I knew I was ready to fly the Atlantic Ocean. The Water Jump. Tom wasn't so optimistic. "It won't be simple. You'll have to carry a whacking load of fuel. The weather in autumn is against you. You'll be alone for a night and a day. No radio—and no one to hear you if you had one. If you misjudge anything, you'll end up in the water."

"You're still acting like my teacher," I accused.

His intelligent blue eyes stared me down. "If you pull this stunt off, you won't be anybody's pupil."

"So you'll help me?"

"Beryl, it won't be easy." He rubbed his hands and began to set up my regimen. "No drinking, no smoking. No late nights. Exercise every day. You'll have to train like an athlete."

And I've trained as hard as I did when I was a child, when my heart's desire was to jump higher than my head. For this challenge, I've left nothing to chance.

CHAPTER NINE

BERYL SHIFTED IN HER BED, WINCING AT THE SORE SPOTS WHERE Simi's throw had landed her against the wall. She willed herself to fall asleep, but something wasn't right. What could it be? The leopard was dead. Simi was dead. Her hut had a sturdy wooden door. Where else could danger come from?

She concentrated, sniffing the air as Arap Maina had taught her. Fresh air was coming in where fresh air had no place to be. Someone or something had moved the flap of cloth hanging across her window opening. Careful not to make a sound, Beryl ran her hand under her mattress for her knife. Suddenly a head blocked the starlight—a long, elegant shaved head.

"Kibii?" Beryl whispered. He had never visited her at night before.

"Who else?" Her friend's low voice was matter-of-fact, almost surprised that she had asked. "Come out. The dancing will start soon."

Beryl threw off the spread, pulled the mosquito netting aside, and reached into the crate next to her bed for khaki shorts and a dark shirt. Buller rolled over on his back and began to snore.

"You always were a lousy watchdog," she whispered. "Sleep well, friend. I'll be back later." She picked up her boots and hauled open the heavy wooden door. Beryl inhaled deeply; the cold air was raw in her throat. Kibii's white teeth gleamed in the dark. She grinned back.

"Where are we going?" she asked.

"The Kikuyu village. There's a *ngoma*," he replied. He glanced at the boots in her hand and shook his head. "Your shoes will make too much noise."

Beryl had always wanted to go to one of the native dances. She dropped the boots.

Suddenly a child's cry cracked the night. Beryl and Kibii shrank against the wall of the hut, peering toward the main house. Squares of light floated in the darkness. Beryl realized it was not as late as she had thought; her father and Emma were still awake.

"It's Little A," Beryl whispered. "Even though Simi is dead, he's still scared."

"Is it true you killed the baboon with one blow?"

"Two," Beryl admitted. "After the first one, I thought he was dead—there was so much blood."

"Dead animals don't bleed," he reminded her.

"Everything happened so fast, I forgot," she admitted. "But my second blow finished him."

"You did what needed to be done." Grudging as it was, it was still praise. "It was something I might have done." He held his hand to his ear. "The Kikuyu music will start soon. I think you will like their dancing."

"I've never been to their village." Beryl hesitated. The Kikuyu performed the farm's most backbreaking labor. They lived a few miles away on the edge of the forest. It was a long way to go in the night. "I'm forbidden to go out alone."

"If I go with you, then you are not alone," Kibii said logically.

"That's true."

Kibii took off. Beryl forgot her qualms and soon caught up with him. They loped down into the valley with the gait peculiar to Kibii's people that the settlers called "hop and carry one." Beryl had never run faster. It was as if the crisp evening air was propelling her forward. The moon was full, and lit their path better than lanterns could. Even the mysterious noises—the strange animal calls, the crackling of branches, the rustling underfoot—held no fear for her tonight. She was Beru, and she had defended her tribe against the enemy. Her arms swung wider and her stride lengthened.

Finally, with the village just in sight, she stopped and stood still, breathing hard.

Kibii still had his wind. "Beru, you have to train harder," he scolded. "A *murani* does not pant. Your prey would be gone before you caught your breath."

Chest aching, Beryl breathed heavily through her nose. Shaking his head, Kibii walked past her toward the village of mud and brush huts.

"I didn't think you liked the Kikuyu," Beryl whispered to Kibii.

"I do not. They have looked to the earth for so long, they cannot see the sky."

"Daddy says they farm well and don't cause any trouble."

He snorted. "That's why I do not like them."

Beryl and Kibii joined the other children, both Nandi and Kikuyu, at one end of the large clearing where the dancing was to take place. There were sidelong glances at them, particularly at Beryl, who shook her head defiantly, her blond braids catching the firelight. Grudgingly, room was made for them.

In the clearing, young men stood together in a wide circle with their arms on each other's shoulders. One man stood in the center, the leader. Anticipation rippled through the audience.

"What's he going to do?" Beryl whispered to Kibii.

"Wait." Kibii never took his eyes off the dancer inside the circle.

The leader suddenly leapt into the air. At the top of the jump, he waggled his shoulders. He looked like a bird ruffling his feathers in midflight. He opened his mouth and hurled his chant at the others like a challenge. They accepted, and the music swelled from one to the other until they were all singing the same sounds. Beryl thought it sounded like one person's voice, repeated and overlaid twentyfold. And all the while, the leader was leaping, setting the rhythm.

The circle of dancers began to stomp, daring him to jump faster and higher. Beryl and Kibii were stomping the beat like the others, the music infecting their blood. The leader's head rocked back and forth on top of his rigid neck. His toes stretched impossibly long toward the ground, touching the dirt only for an instant before flying again.

Finally, Kibii stirred. "Ahh," he said. "He is tiring."

Beryl looked closely and saw that the leader's leaps were not quite so high. Although he still sang out the chant, the sinews in his chest were drawn like cords, and he dragged in deep breaths on every down stroke. Then he faltered. His misstep shuddered through the music. Beryl felt as though cold water had been splashed on her. Before the leader could miss another beat, another dancer stepped forward, taking his place. The first leader leapt his last leap and stopped dead. His head bowed, shame in the set of his shoulders, he moved outside the circle.

"He wasn't strong enough," Beryl said, feeling exhausted, as though she had led the dancing.

"He failed," Kibii said.

The dancing would continue until dawn, but Beryl and Kibii slipped away while it was still dark. As they walked, they talked about the dancing and how funny it was that the serious Kikuyu danced so well.

"Daddy tried to count them for the government again last week, but the tribe thinks it's unlucky," Beryl said. "They shuffled around so he couldn't get a good number."

Kibii answered, "Why he does he want to know how many there are?"

"He told me that the government worries about native revolts."

"The Kikuyu?" Kibii asked, his eyes wide.

Beryl nodded, laughing. "Daddy thinks the same. He says that they can't be bothered to fight for anyone, least of all themselves." She paused. "I wonder if he has ever seen them dance."

They walked in a companionable silence until they reached a bit of clearing with a fine view of the valley. They stopped to admire the landscape rolled out below them like an Oriental carpet. The stars overhead were brilliant against the black sky.

"This is good," Beryl said.

"Yes."

"I'd like to fly over the valley, like an eagle."

Kibii shook his head. "What good would that do? You cannot know the land until you walk it."

"You could see everything if you flew."

"Since you cannot fly, it does not matter."

Beryl reflected for a moment. "The dancers looked as though they could fly. I wish I could dance like that." She began to leap, slowly at first, then higher and faster, like a fledgling trying out her wings.

Kibii watched carefully. "No, Beru. You are pushing off with the ball of your foot. You must use your toes! Like this." And he began to leap too.

Beryl was so intent on lifting herself higher than Kibii that she didn't hear the sound of men. Suddenly, lanterns blinded her.

"We've found her!" a man cried in Dutch-accented English. It was one of her father's Boer foremen. He grabbed her arm. "Little missy—we've been looking for you half the night."

"Run, Kibii!" she shouted.

Midleap, Kibii twisted his body and flung himself into the trees. In an instant he was gone.

Beryl's feet, which moments earlier had flown over the forest path, felt like lead. The foreman held her arm, not too roughly, all the way to her father's house. All the windows were lit, and the

Captain was pacing on the porch. Arthur was sitting on the stoop, his arms wrapped around his knees, tears streaming down his cheeks. His face cleared as soon as he saw Beryl.

"You're back!" he cried. "I thought you were dead in the woods!"

"I'm fine, Arthur." She straightened her back and waited for her father to say something. He stared at her for a few moments, his face a block of stone. With deliberate slowness, he pulled out his watch, glanced at the time, and replaced it in its special pocket in his vest. Then he called into the house, "Emma, we've found her."

Emma appeared in the doorway, carrying a paraffin lantern. She wore a lacy nightdress, belted tightly around her waist. She looked like a porcelain doll with her blond curls and violet eyes.

"Thank goodness." She glimpsed Beryl and her face became even paler. "Where have you been? Don't you know how worried we've been? First Arthur and that awful creature, then . . ."

The foreman and his men stared openly at Emma's nightdress. The Captain brushed past Beryl to dismiss them to their huts. Then he turned his attention back to his household. "Everyone inside."

Arthur said, "Can I stay up to hear you yell at Beryl?"

The Captain swung Arthur across his back. "Off to bed with you, young man."

"Dad, I have bad dreams."

"He's not your dad," Beryl said.

"Beryl, shut your mouth. It doesn't matter." Then her father asked in a gentle voice that Beryl didn't recognize, "What kind of dreams, son?"

"Son?" Beryl repeated under her breath.

"My brains were getting eaten by a bear," Arthur said.

"Arthur, that's nonsense," Emma said.

"No, it's not," Beryl spat. "There's a bear in the forest that eats the brains of its prey. I told Arthur all about it."

A small, vexed cry escaped Emma's lips.

"Arthur, the bear doesn't like boy brains," the Captain said, glaring at his daughter. "They're too tough. Now, women's brains . . . they're soft and mushy."

Arthur giggled.

"Emma," the Captain said, handing Arthur to his mother, "put him to bed."

"I'll be back, and we *will* discuss this," Emma said darkly as she led Arthur away.

Beryl and her father were alone in the Captain's long living room. Beryl kept her eyes on her dirt-encrusted toes, but she could feel her father's stare on the top of her head. A cedar fire crackled and spat in the large stone fireplace. Emma's influence was everywhere, from the lace doilies on the tables to the decanters on the sideboard. She had even imported a silver soda siphon so the Captain could have his favorite whiskey and soda. The room was filled with light from sputtering oil lamps on every table, as if Emma were trying to keep the darkness at bay.

The Captain sighed and went to pour some whiskey into his cut-crystal glass. Beryl heard the whooshing sound of the soda being added.

"At ease," he finally said.

Beryl relaxed a fraction.

"Why can't you just stay out of trouble?" He rubbed the bridge of his nose between his thumb and forefinger, a mannerism Beryl had seen before when he didn't know what to do with her. "Emma went to check on you tonight. She was worried about you!" His laughter was like a hyena's bark. "Then she's in hysterics, thinking you've been stolen by Gypsies who left your shoes on the stoop or some such nonsense. I had to wake up the men to look for you. Tomorrow, they'll all be exhausted."

"I wasn't in trouble, Daddy. I went to see the Kikuyu dance."

"You should have been in bed, not out wandering alone."

"I wasn't alone," Beryl said.

"Really?" His eyebrows lifted. "Kibii, I suppose. Maybe it was a mistake to let you spend so much time with the Nandi. I can't afford to be distracted." He gestured toward his desk, covered with his training ledgers. Emma's hysterics must have interrupted his nightly record-keeping of his thoroughbreds' progress.

"But Daddy, I've learned so much. Without Arap Maina's training, I never could have killed Simi."

At the pained expression on his face, Beryl fell silent.

They heard Emma's embroidered slippers swishing on the polished wood floor. She sat down at the table that served as the Captain's desk. "Clutt, what are we going to do about the children?"

"Emma, don't be so dramatic. They're both fine."

"Arthur is still suffering shock from this afternoon." Emma shuddered and drew her dressing gown closer.

"Nonsense." The Captain turned his back on her and prodded the fire with a poker.

"Arthur was nearly killed. He saw your daughter beat an animal to death." She shot Beryl an accusing look.

"Why are you blaming Beryl? I'd think you'd be grateful to her for saving Arthur's life," the Captain said.

Beryl felt an unexpected warmth on her face.

"I can't help wondering why Arthur was playing with that creature in the first place," Emma said. "It's not like him."

Beryl guiltily shifted her weight from one foot to another. The Captain glanced at her and began to pace.

"Clutt, she's running wild." Emma's complaints followed him around the room. "Tonight she was out in the woods doing who knows what! She needs a governess."

"Not this again."

"This is no life for an English girl. She's becoming a savage. She doesn't even wear shoes."

Beryl wiggled her bare toes.

"What's next?" Emma asked, watching the Captain shrewdly. "Shaving her head? Piercing her earlobes with wood?"

The Captain ran his finger around his collar and wouldn't meet Emma's eyes. He harrumphed and sat down at his desk.

Emma continued, "A proper governess would be the making of her."

Beryl held herself perfectly still, like a lioness crouched in the grass. If she had had a tail, the tip would have been twitching.

"Beryl is fine," the Captain protested. "She's healthy and eats well."

"She's not one of your horses, darling."

"She handles horses as well as any of the lads in the stable." His gaze wandered back to his ledgers.

"She's not one of the lads, either." Emma sat across from him and tapped the ledger to get his complete attention. "She's eleven years old and she cannot read."

"Nonsense. We read together all the time."

"I mean something more challenging than the racing papers!" Her voice became soft and persuasive. "Don't you want better for her?"

"She should get some schooling, I suppose . . ." he said finally, "but I'd rather spend the money on a new head lad."

"After she's been educated, she could help you with the farm." Emma leaned forward and caught his hand in hers. "It would save you money in the long run."

The Captain absently rubbed the palm of her hand with his callused thumb. "I always assumed she would go back to England to school," he admitted.

"Please, no, Daddy." Neither the Captain nor Emma paid any attention to Beryl's whisper.

Emma sniffed, a tiny, ladylike sound. "Can you imagine Beryl in an English school? She won't even live in a proper house! You must hire a governess." She held his gaze until he reluctantly nodded.

"All right. I'll see to it when I go to the races next month."

"Or you can go on tomorrow's train."

The Captain was startled. "Tomorrow?"

"Tomorrow." Emma was implacable.

"Daddy! No!" Beryl's voice came out in a wail. "I have Arap Maina. I don't need a governess. Emma doesn't know anything!"

"Beryl Clutterbuck, mind your tongue," her father ordered. "I've made my decision."

Beryl shivered; she knew better than to argue with her father when he used that tone.

Emma smiled a satisfied smile, just like Camiscan's smug expression when he terrorized the stable lads.

Clenching and unclenching her fists, Beryl cried, "I'll never forgive you for this, you . . . witch!"

"Beryl!" Emma gasped.

"I'll be here long after you. You'll run away, just like my mother did. Daddy will *never* marry you."

Emma recoiled as though she had been slapped.

"Beryl, go to your hut," the Captain ordered. "And this time, stay there, or God help me, you'll regret it."

Beryl whirled around and left through the wide doorway. The open door spilled a pool of lamplight into the night; at the light's edge, the darkness was even deeper than before. There was no sound except the buzzing of cicadas. Without hesitating, Beryl walked into the dark. From the doorway of her hut, she looked back at the house. Her father's silhouette stood motionless on the porch, watching her.

I'm waiting at the window, watching for a sunrise to appear through the drizzle. The telephone peals its shrill noise.

"Beryl Markham?" the familiar sour voice asks.

"Yes." I hold my breath. Any more delay, and the autumn storms will stop me before I begin.

"Low clouds and thunder again today. Possibly a break in the late afternoon. But behind that is a strong gale."

"How far behind? How much time do I have?"

"We don't know." The voice hesitates. "Mrs. Markham, the Air Ministry strongly advises against this flight. No one has managed a solo flight from Britain to New York."

"That's why I'm doing it."

There is a disapproving cough on the other end of the line. "Of the last ten who tried, one ditched, one turned back, three crashed, and the last five disappeared.

This late in the year, the headwinds will be stronger than ever. It can't be done, least of all by a woman."

Looking out the window, I catch a glimpse of lighter sky. "I'm going this afternoon, come what may."

"The Air Ministry cannot take responsibility."

"I wouldn't expect you to. But I promised Lord Carberry I'd get his plane back for the October races. I never break a promise."

After a moment, the voice says, "If you insist on going . . ."

"I do."

"Then . . . Godspeed."

This is my chance. By this time tomorrow, I'll either be the first to do the Water Jump, east to west. . . . Or I'll be dead.

At least it won't be dull.

CHAPTER TEN

"WAKE UP, BERYL," THE CAPTAIN BELLOWED. HE POUNDED ON HER door with his fist.

Beryl's eyes flew open. She stared at her thatch roof, feeling grateful she finally had a wooden door. Her second thought followed quickly: What a shame she had never gotten around to making a back door to her *rondavel*.

"How angry do you think he is?" she whispered to Buller. The dog snorted and rolled over.

The Captain pounded again. "Beryl, I know you're in there."

She scrambled out of bed and threw on one of the togas Kibii's mother had made for her. Wiping the sleep from her eyes, she swung open the door.

"Yes, Daddy?" she asked, shivering. The dew on the hard mud floor was ice-cold and she shifted her weight from one foot to another, rubbing her bare arms to keep warm.

Even though his eyes were tired and shadowed, her father did not look furious.

"Look at you—Emma would say that butter wouldn't melt in your mouth," her father said with a wry grin. The tightness in her chest loosened. "As if I'd forget your behavior last night."

"I'm sorry," Beryl said.

"Good. And I expect you to apologize to Emma, too . . . nicely." He looked her over and shook his head. "For God's sake, get some proper clothes on. I've a train to catch."

"To Nairobi? I can come?" Beryl's breath caught at the possibility. Her father occasionally let her accompany him to the only city she had ever known. Even if she had to return with a governess, the train ride down would be hers and his together. Alone.

"Ha! You think after last night I would take you to Nairobi? No, you'll ride with me as far as Nakuru, then you can take the horses back with the post." He pulled out his pocket watch. "Step to it, Beryl; we'll leave in exactly twenty minutes."

A few hours later she was mounted on Wee McGregor, the Arabian pony her father had given her years ago to learn to ride. The stirrups were lengthened as far as they could go, and still her legs were too long for the pony. The Captain rode the Baron, a retired cavalry charger. The Captain permitted no one else to ride him.

The only conversation was her father's barked instructions: "Beryl, your heels are pointing out— what good does that do you or the horse?" or "Beryl, for God's sake, loosen up on the reins before you snap that pony's neck." Beryl kept her mouth shut, obeyed her father's orders, and brooded about governesses.

They were startled by a white stork gliding over their heads. The bird flapped its enormous wings and began to climb. The Captain reined in and shielded his eyes to watch. The stork's feathers shimmered and melted in the merciless morning sun. Beryl waited, curious. It wasn't often that her father took the time to appreciate any animals other than his precious thoroughbreds.

When the stork was only a speck in the cloudless sky, the Captain sighed. "Beryl, have I ever told you about Daedalus and his son Icarus?"

Beryl cast her mind back to all the myths her father had regaled her with when she was little. "I don't think so."

"Daedalus was an inventor who was imprisoned on the island of Crete. Daedalus decided the only way he could escape was to fly."

"Fly? In ancient Greece?" Beryl asked.

Her father smiled. "He designed two sets of wings made of feathers and wax. One for himself and one for Icarus, his son. Icarus couldn't wait to fly, but his father warned him not to fly too high."

"Did they work?" Beryl asked, rolling her shoulders as though she were wearing wings.

"They did. They escaped and headed toward the mainland. But Icarus was reckless. He flew faster and higher than his father. So high, he couldn't hear his father's warnings." The Captain glared at Beryl.

"What happened?" Beryl asked in a small voice.

"The sun melted his wings and Icarus fell into the sea. He drowned."

"Daddy, that's an awful story!"

He watched her closely. "Perhaps. But there was a lesson in it. Do you understand it?"

Beryl thought. Finally she said, "If I ever fly, it won't be with wax wings."

The Captain laughed, but Beryl could see the worry in his eyes.

After a few miles, the Captain tried again. "Beryl, I know you aren't happy, but a governess will be good for you."

Beryl had been waiting for this. "But Daddy, I don't need one," she cried. "You would never think I did if it weren't for that blasted wo—"

The Captain reached over and slapped her leg. Hard. She clamped her teeth together to keep from crying out.

His forbidding face relaxed slightly. "At least Arap Maina is teaching you some discipline. A shame he can't teach you manners," he said.

"He's ever so strict; he'd never let me talk that way." Too late she saw his trap.

Her father's narrow lips stretched in a quick grin. "Beryl, Arap Maina taught you how to behave among the Nandi. But now you must learn to behave among the British. *We* are your people."

Beryl straightened up on her pony, eyes fixed on the tangled trees on either side of the narrow track ahead. For a thousand years Kibii's people had carved a narrow path, just wide enough for a bull to pass, but the determined wagons of the British settlers had made it wider and permanent.

"You'll see. I'll bring back someone nice," the Captain went on. "Someone young, who can teach you to be a proper lady, since you refuse to learn from Emma."

"Daddy, tell me one thing, just one thing, that a *governess*," she hissed the end of the word like a mamba might, "could teach me about surviving here."

The Captain harrumphed. "She'll teach you to get along with the other girls. Every time you meet my friends' daughters, you turn up your nose as if they smell bad."

"Daddy, they do! All perfume and soap."

"They smell like young ladies."

"None of them have visited since Emma came," Beryl said thoughtfully. "Maybe the girls don't like Emma either."

"Never mind that." The Captain's neck reddened. "We're talking about you. Would it be such a sacrifice to wear a dress once in a while?"

"You can't want me to dress like those girls. I wouldn't last five minutes in the bush."

Her father let out an amused grunt and resettled himself in the saddle. "Beryl, when will you understand that I don't intend for you to 'survive' in the bush? Next month, I'm buying a second steam engine. I'll have another hundred acres cleared by summer. I'm going to be a rich man. So you, my dear, have to learn to act like a girl with expectations."

"I expect the worst!" Beryl said in a mournful voice.

"I know you do." He laughed. "And that's my fault. If I hadn't been so busy with the farm, you'd have had a more British upbringing. This was supposed to be Emma's job. No white girl should be raised by the Nandi."

"I thought you admired the Nandi."

"The way I respect a fine horse. They're magnificent specimens." He patted the Baron's withers. "But the best stallions are always a little wild and not to be trusted. Especially with your education." His speech had gotten louder, startling the wild monkeys hanging in the trees along the road. The brightly colored kingfisher and bee-eater birds flew up in squawking anger, blotting out the sun.

"Kibii's my friend!" Beryl protested. "And Arap Maina is the finest teacher in Africa!"

"They're not civilized," he corrected. "No matter how much we like them, Beryl, we must never forget that we are the superior race. This is our continent now."

The monkeys shrieked and began swinging away from the track. A tremor went through Beryl's body, like a horse's hide shivering to dislodge a fly. Her father was wrong about Arap Maina and Kibii. All the British settlers put together were of no use to her. Only the Nandi understood her.

Arriving at the wooden platform with its corrugated iron roof, they dismounted without stiffness, even though they had been riding for several hours. The last time she had been here was six months ago when Camiscan arrived. And Emma.

The Captain handed Beryl his reins. "Where is the blasted train?" he demanded, glancing at his pocket watch. "How are we going to build the Empire if the train is always late?"

Beryl shrugged; she had never known the train to arrive on time. On a good day, the noisy engine might travel ten miles an hour, assuming an animal had not wandered onto the track.

"After you get the mail, head straight home," the Captain ordered. "No dawdling. And don't worry Emma while I'm gone."

Sourly, Beryl agreed. "If *you* say so."

The Captain grabbed her chin and gripped it tight between his callused thumb and forefinger. "Young lady, I do say so. If you don't learn some manners soon, I'll tan your hide with my belt." He took a deep breath, released her chin, and sighed. "Beryl, what has Emma ever done to you?"

"That woman is not my mother." Beryl's face burned as though he had branded her with his fingers, but she refused to cry.

He let out an exasperated sigh and rubbed the bridge of his nose. "No one said she was, but your mother is gone. She ran away to England with that major with the wooden teeth. She hated Africa more than she loved us. Don't you see that?"

Beryl didn't answer.

"Please do your best to get along with Emma," he said. "She's working like the devil to make a home for us."

"Where's her husband, anyway?"

He squinted as he stared down the tracks. "For all intents and purposes, Orchardson abandoned Emma and Arthur." Almost pleading, he said, "Don't you see? Emma and I are both alone."

"You aren't alone. You have me!" Beryl muttered.

"Beryl, Emma is here to stay. Try to be nice." He cleared his throat. With relief, they both identified the unmistakable metallic clacking of the train approaching the station. A long, slow hiss and it groaned to a halt.

"Look, Beryl, there's Lord Delamere. I want to talk to him about the mill. Be a good girl and run along now."

Lord D., as everyone called him, had sponsored Captain Clutterbuck when he first arrived in British East Africa. The Captain gave Beryl an absent-minded kiss as he turned to greet his patron. Beryl was left alone on the platform, holding the reins to both horses.

Beryl collected the post, mainly letters for Emma and horse-breeding catalogs for her father. She pulled Wee McGregor's head around toward home and led the Baron behind her. As soon as she was out of sight of the train station, she dismounted Wee McGregor and leapt onto the Baron's back.

Once back at Green Hills, she unsaddled the horses and was careful to leave the stables by the back way to avoid Emma. Arthur's voice startled her.

"Hi, Beryl!" he said cheerfully. He'd been lying in wait for her.

"Don't sneak up on me like that!" Beryl said. "I've been trained— you don't know what I might do."

"I bet Dad doesn't know you rode the Baron. He'd be mad. But I won't tell. Do you want to play?"

She stared at the raw slashes on his face. "Do those hurt?" she asked.

"Like the dickens!" he bragged cheerfully. "I was nearly killed!"

Beryl cringed. "Look, Little A—" She took a deep breath and said in a rush, "I'm really sorry. What happened yesterday was my fault. I shouldn't have told you to play with Simi."

Arthur was silent for a few moments. Then he beamed up at Beryl. "But then you saved me." He stuck out his hand. "We're even."

"That's decent of you." Beryl shook his hand and turned to leave. "I have to go to the village."

He grabbed her arm. "Take me with you, please. Please!" Arthur was not allowed to visit the village, but that never stopped him from begging to go with her.

"Little A, you know I can't." With luck, she would be in time for one of Arap Maina's lessons.

"Just this once?" he pleaded. "I'll bring the mail up to the house for you." Arthur looked up at her with a puppy's longing eyes.

"Maybe next time. But you have to practice your jumping while I am gone."

"I will, I will." Arthur sprang up and down enthusiastically as Beryl watched with a critical eye.

"Not like that! Your toes must stretch downward. You must believe you can fly." Beryl began to leap straight up, gaining more height with each leap. Arthur's delighted laughter helped her spring even higher.

"Beryl, I think you did it that time. You jumped over your head." He was still jumping, and his words puffed out to coincide with his landings.

Beryl was pleased, too, even if she wouldn't admit it. "Maybe I did, but only because I practice all the time. See that you do, too. I'm going now."

Leaving Arthur bouncing in place as if his life depended on it, she loped toward the village. She had to find Arap Maina.

The Nandi village had grown in the past year. Now there were several dozen huts arranged in two circles, one inside the other to protect the cattle. Beryl waved at the women with their colorful red *shukas* and their beaded necklaces that extended in collars as wide as their shoulders. She gave a huge smile to Kibii's other mother, Naipende, who was her favorite.

"Hello, Naipende. Working as hard as ever?"

"Greetings, Beru. Who else will prepare the meals, or build the house, or care for the children?"

"Not the boys!" Beryl laughed. "They hunt to get away from women's work."

"And you have always preferred to be with them. The women still remember your thatching." Naipende burst out laughing. "The boys are at the other side of the meadow."

Beryl thanked her and set off at a run. The boys stood in a circle around Arap Maina. His thick hair was captured in narrow plaits that hung down to the small of his back. Today his bracelets were gold, green, and red, tied high and tight on his forearm. His toga was knotted at his shoulder; his chest was bare to show off his iron cable necklace. Beryl's father said that whenever the government tried to build a telegraph line, giraffes knocked down the poles and the Africans stole the wire for jewelry. As far as Beryl was concerned, the lack of telegraph service to Green Hills was a small price to pay for Arap Maina's splendid necklace.

Arap Maina spoke quietly, with authority. How could her father think of him as an animal?

He asked his students to identify the dung on the ground.

"Gazelle?" suggested Kibii, with a doubtful voice.

"No."

"Water buffalo." It was Mehru, a boy who was always trying to impress Arap Maina.

Arap Maina shook his head. "That is no buffalo dropping. Look more closely."

Obediently, the boys hopped into a tighter circle.

"The shape is wrong. Feel the wetness; smell it. All of you should know lion spoor. The cattle are in danger." To the Nandi, there was no greater threat. The boys were training to be *murani*, the guardians of the tribe's wealth, its cattle.

"Tomorrow the *murani* will hunt this lion," Arap Maina said.

Beryl caught her breath as an excited murmur rose from the boys. Every warrior longed to prove himself against the greatest enemy. Legends were born during lion hunts.

"We should sharpen our spears," said Mehru.

"We should pray to Enka that we take down the lion in one blow!" said another.

"Ha! This is warriors' work," laughed Arap Maina. But the smile in his eyes told Beryl that he was proud of their courage. "Your work is to find a healthy bull for the ceremony. He must not have any blemishes."

Beryl seized her moment. "Arap Maina, I would like to go on the hunt." Her words fell into a shocked silence. Arap Maina had often taken the young people hunting for small game, but a lion hunt was serious business.

Behind his father, Kibii bent over laughing. Beryl scowled at him, already afraid she was making a fool of herself.

"Beru, only the *murani* hunt lion." Arap Maina's lips twitched.

"I know, but I can take care of myself." Beryl dug her toes into the soft ground.

"What can a white girl do on a hunt?" It was Mehru who taunted her. Arap Maina silenced him with a glance.

"I have not taught you to defend yourself against a lion," Arap Maina said sternly. "I never thought you would be foolish enough to hunt one."

"I am ready," she insisted.

He shook his head.

"Arap Maina, my father wants me to go on a hunt," Beryl said deliberately, as though he was hard of hearing. She gulped and went on, "He insists."

"I will ask him myself," Arap Maina replied, glancing at the boys.

"He's in Nairobi," Beryl answered. "Do you doubt what I say?"

After a long moment, Arap Maina shrugged. "You may go only if you promise to obey my orders. I swore an oath to your father that I would keep you safe."

"I promise." She glanced around the boys and quickly dropped her eyes. She couldn't bear to see the shocked disbelief on Kibii's face and the sullen anger on Mehru's.

I exit the hangar. There's the low roar of a heavy plane above us, a bomber. It looks like a fat marabou stork gliding in for a landing. Bombers are ugly planes; they handle as though they're flying through treacle.

My ground crew is waiting impatiently by my lovely new plane, <u>The Messenger</u>. Suddenly, I hear a loud boom and the ground shakes. The bomber has crashed. We all start to run toward the burning hulk of metal. The smoke billows from its carcass. We're all watching for the same thing: Did the pilot survive?

A voice at my shoulder startles me. It's my engine mechanic, Josh. "We'll have to wait for that to be cleared before you can take off," he says.

I nod, but my eyes are locked on the smoldering cockpit. "I hope you're not superstitious," he says. "That can't be a good sign."

"We all know the dangers," I reply. "A landing can go either way."

Something's happening . . . shouting and frantic activity at the cockpit. The pilot stumbles onto the tarmac. There's the wailing siren of an ambulance. He's being helped onto a wheeled cot. Better that than a hearse.

"Whew, that's a relief," I say. "Let's get started. I've got an ocean to cross."

CHAPTER ELEVEN

BERYL RAN FULL TILT DOWN THE STEEP PATH TOWARD THE village. The valley spread out in front of her, shimmering in the pearly light just before dawn. Her feet slipping on the small rocks, she spread her arms wide just to keep her balance. When she hit the flat part of the trail, she settled into a steady jog. The hunters would be gathering at the Nandi village soon. She circled a stand of acacia trees and stopped short. Kibii was standing there. The expression on his face made her stomach twist.

"Kibii! What's wrong?" Beryl cried.

"You should be ashamed of yourself." His voice was low and angry. "You don't belong on a hunt."

"Why not?" Beryl shot back.

"You are only pretending to be a warrior. You have not trained. You could be hurt or killed."

"I'm trained well enough." Beryl tried to sound confident. "Kibii,

I'll be all right. Your father will look after me." She reached out to pat his shoulder.

Kibii recoiled from her hand. "He may get hurt because he has to look after you!"

"Is that why you're upset? You're worried about Arap Maina?"

"No, of course not." Kibii bristled at the insult to his family. "He is a great warrior."

"Then what's the problem?" she asked, exasperated.

"You used to respect our traditions. But now you are just like the other settlers. You take what you want." Kibii stared at her with his dark eyes. Beryl was shocked to see that he was almost in tears.

She shifted from foot to foot, tugging on her braid.

"You should have to wait, like me!" Kibii burst out. He turned away, his straight back rigid with anger.

"If I don't have to wait, then neither should you," Beryl said eagerly. "What if I ask your father . . .?"

Kibii gave her a withering look. "Beru, you can make up your own rules, but I cannot. Besides, my father would never let me go. I will not go after the lion for two more seasons."

"I'm really sorry," she said.

"You say you want to be like me, but I would never do what you are doing."

"I said I was sorry, but I'm going on that hunt." She was beginning to get angry herself. "You would do the same if you could."

Kibii shook his head. "It's not just me who is angry. All the boys are. Mehru is the worst of all; you've made an enemy."

"He never liked me. But what about you? Are you still my friend?" Beryl asked in a small voice.

"I haven't decided yet." He turned his back on her and headed for the village. She followed, but her feet felt heavy.

They arrived at Arap Maina's hut as the pink of the sunrise appeared over the mountains and the valley began to emerge from its nighttime shadows. The village dogs greeted them with their wet noses and wagging tails. She thought regretfully of Buller, left asleep in her hut. She wished he were here. The village had suddenly become a place full of strangers speaking a foreign language.

Arap Maina's wives were preparing the fire. Naipende nodded to Beryl in greeting, and Namasari gave her a piece of fruit. From their silence, Beryl knew that they, too, disapproved.

Arap Maina stood in the doorway of his hut, waiting for them. Kibii nodded stiffly to his father. Arap Maina patted the boy's shoulder. "Kibii, you may blood the ox."

Kibii's eyes lit up. This was a worthy task. He nodded eagerly and ran toward the cattle enclosure in the center of the kraal. Beryl started after him, but Arap Maina stopped her with a gesture of his hand.

"No, Beru. Women do not touch the ox before a hunt. It is forbidden." A shadow passed over Arap Maina's face, and Beryl knew he was thinking that girls do not hunt either. But he said nothing.

As they waited, Arap Maina prepared for the hunting ritual by breathing deeply, standing on one leg. To Beryl, he seemed to be in a trance. She lifted her right leg, but her left leg seemed to have a mind of its own. Hoping Arap Maina wouldn't notice, she switched from one foot to the other.

She caught a glimpse of two brown eyes staring at her from inside Arap Maina's hut. It was Kibii's older sister, Jebbta.

Glancing warily at her father, whose eyes were half-closed, Jebbta came out. She grabbed Beryl's hand and pulled her around the back of the hut.

"Hello, Jebbta," Beryl said warily.

"Beru, go home." Jebbta wore an ankle-length skirt made of zebra skin and had sticks of wood pierced through her upper ear. Her many bracelets jingled as she moved. She spent all her time trying to attract the attention of the boys, particularly Mehru.

"I'm tired of everyone saying that," Beryl said.

"You don't have the courage to hunt with the *murani*. Mehru says you will be killed. And your father will blame the tribe. He'll demand a blood price, and we will lose all our cattle," the dark girl said.

"Don't be ridiculous, Jebbta," Beryl muttered. "My father would never do that. Anyway, I'll be fine."

"It is you who are being ridiculous," Jebbta said earnestly. "Your body is like mine, no stronger. You will hold them back."

"Just watch me!" Turning her back on Jebbta, Beryl walked back to Arap Maina. She was startled to see another warrior standing beside him. He towered over Beryl, and his chest was crisscrossed with scars. He handled his spear as though it were another limb.

Arap Maina announced, "Beru, this is Tepli. You will stay with him during the hunt. Behind the *murani*."

"But," Beryl protested. "I want to hunt with everyone else."

Tepli was even more disgusted than Beryl. "Arap Maina, I am no nursemaid! It dishonors me." He looked down his nose at Beryl.

Arap Maina held up a hand. "Beru, if you want to come, you will do as I say. Tepli, it is your duty to protect the daughter of

Cluttabucki." He stared until both Beryl and Tepli reluctantly nodded.

Tepli removed his *shuka* from his shoulder and tied it around his waist. He wore only a loincloth under the scarlet cloth.

Beryl felt herself reddening, and stared at her bare feet.

A few moments later Kibii returned, leading a healthy reddish-brown ox with a rhino-hide halter. He was flanked by the warriors who were hunting that day. Arap Maina signaled to Jebbta, and she scurried forward to hand him an arrow and a gourd. The arrow's shaft had a block of wood a fingertip's length from the arrowhead. Arap Maina nodded to the other warriors to keep the ox still. Beryl crowded forward with the rest, her eyes wide to see everything.

The ox moaned when Arap Maina punctured its neck with a swift jab of the arrow. The block of wood kept it from penetrating too deeply and killing the beast. Kibii ran in with the gourd and placed it to catch the blood. When the gourd was half full, Arap Maina removed the arrow, and another man quickly wrapped the bull's neck to stop the bleeding. Mehru, puffed up with his own importance, led the lowing beast away, back to the herd.

Jebbta added curdled milk to the gourd. Kibii mixed it and brought it back to Arap Maina, who held it up to the rising sun.

"Praise Enka for the blood, which brings strength to our loins," he chanted.

Beryl glanced at the sinewy legs of the *murani*. The thin red togas strapped to their bodies barely covered their private parts. She looked down at her own scrawny legs, poking out like sticks encased in baggy khaki shorts.

Arap Maina took a deep swallow of the blood and milk. Then he handed the gourd to Tepli, who said, "By the sacred womb of my mother, we will kill the wild lion today." He looked down at Beryl with dislike and deliberately passed the gourd over her head to the warrior standing on her other side.

Beryl didn't protest; her stomach was already roiling.

Without warning, Kibii was at her side, handing her a lightweight spear. "I hope to Enka you do not need this," he whispered.

She touched the blade at the end of the spear with her fingertips. "Thanks, Kibii," she whispered back, but he had already moved away.

Arap Maina pumped his fist in the air. The tall warriors began to move out, the sun glinting off their spears. The women and children shouted cries of encouragement.

Kibii and Mehru were standing off to the side, glaring at Beryl. She tightened her hold on her new spear and followed the *murani* into battle.

Flash. Pop.

My eyes are blinded by a photographer's bulb. No doubt the evening papers will have a caption: "Society blonde wears a no-nonsense Burberry, gray flannel trousers, and a jaunty white hat as she sets off for her transatlantic air flight." As if it matters what I wear!

I deliberately turn my back on the press to say good-bye to my friends.

Josh, my engine mechanic, gives me a sprig of heather.

Brian, who has helped me train for the flight, gives me the newest lifesaving device, a pneumatic jacket I can inflate through a rubber tube. "You could float around in it for days," he says. But I have to decide between carrying the weight of the lifesaver or a warm sweater. If I go down, the jacket will just prolong the inevitable. I choose the sweater.

Finally, Jim Mollison, a pilot who has crossed the Atlantic twice and a staunch friend, lends me his watch. I'll set mine to GMT and set his to New York time. If . . . <u>when</u> I arrive, the time change might be disorientating.

Jim grins at me as I strap his watch on my wrist. "Don't get it wet!"

CHAPTER TWELVE

BERYL PLACED HER FEET AS QUIETLY AS SHE COULD, AWARE THAT Tepli's hostile ears were listening and judging every step. She was determined to prove that she could hold her own with the *murani*, that she, too, had wings on her ankles. Thinking hard about being light on her feet, she forgot where she was stepping. Her heel landed on a pat of cattle dung and she nearly lost her footing.

"Ugh!" she exclaimed, wiping her foot on the dry grass. Tepli grabbed her elbow and wrenched her upright. Arap Maina glanced back and scowled.

They ran in single file into the valley. It was the end of the dry season, and the papery grass reached to Beryl's waist. She couldn't help but notice that the grass went only to the knees of the warriors.

Arap Maina led them down a path she couldn't see. The line of hunters swerved to avoid thorn bushes and the rock-hard anthills that towered above their heads. Within an hour they had run farther than Beryl had ever ventured. As they descended deeper into the valley, the sun rose higher in the sky. Waves of heat came up from the valley floor, hitting Beryl in the face like a stone wall. She had a stitch in her side, and every breath she drew hurt her chest.

A bevy of partridges flew up from a copse of trees sticking up from the grassy valley floor. The *murani* froze. Taken by surprise, Beryl would have bumped into the man in front of her if Tepli's iron grip on her shoulder had not held her back.

He glared at her, his eyebrows pulled together high on his bulging forehead. "Watering hole," he said.

"What frightened the birds?" she whispered. "Is it the lion?"

"Ssshh," he hissed.

The warriors stood like statues, muscles tensed, arms halfway raised to the spear-throwing position. Wordlessly, Arap Maina signaled the fastest warriors. They took off at a run, spreading out to either side of the distant watering hole. In a few moments, they disappeared into the haze. Only Arap Maina, Tepli, and Beryl remained.

Beryl looked questioningly at Arap Maina.

He answered quietly, "They flush out our quarry. If he is a lion who runs, they will chase him down."

Beryl hefted her small spear and wondered what use it would be against a lion who runs.

Arap Maina inhaled deeply, his nostrils flaring. "He is there," he said confidently. "But I think he may be a lion who prefers to wait. To attack from a place of concealment."

Beryl gulped at the thought of a lion smart enough to hide. She wished that Arap Maina had not sent away all the warriors.

The three of them advanced cautiously toward the waterhole. Butterflies were everywhere, bumping up against their sweaty bodies.

"Arap Maina, where are the animals who drink this water?" she asked.

"Only the creatures that are safe in the daytime are out today," he whispered.

"There is nothing here," Tepli said sullenly. "The others have found it. I should be with them."

Perspiration ran into Beryl's eyes. She shook her head, disturbing the gnats that seemed to swarm around only her.

"Look there." Arap Maina pointed a long finger to a grassy thicket, on the far side of the watering hole. "Do you see?"

Tepli looked for several moments. A slow smile spread across his face. He nodded, stroking his spear. Beryl screwed up her eyes against the sun and stared. But she could not see what they saw.

"What is it?" she asked around the dryness in her mouth.

"Wait here." Arap Maina carefully placed his shield on the ground. Holding his spear firmly at his side, he began to move forward. Tepli followed.

Beryl grabbed at Tepli's arm. "Don't leave me alone!"

He shook her off, but Arap Maina glanced back. "Tepli, stay with Beru."

"Arap Maina, you cannot face the lion alone," Tepli urged. "You may injure him, but he will kill you. You need me at your back."

"Your duty is to guard Beru."

"My duty is to kill the lion."

"Stay." Arap Maina ran toward the thicket without even looking to see if Tepli obeyed.

Tepli took a few steps after him, glanced back at Beryl, and, with a disgusted growl, returned to her side.

Beryl quietly sighed in relief.

Tepli watched Arap Maina's progress intently, one hand gripping his spear, the other holding his shield of buffalo hide. Beryl shaded her eyes, trying to make out the lion.

"Maybe Arap Maina is wrong?" she asked. Tepli didn't answer.

Without warning, the lion burst out of the cover of the *donga* and charged toward Arap Maina.

Beryl screamed, "Arap Maina, watch out!"

"Eele!" shouted Arap Maina. He hefted his spear to his shoulder. "Eele! Arap Maina!"

To Beryl, it seemed as if the world had slowed to a crawl. The lion floated off the ground, drifting down to earth to push off with its massive paws. Arap Maina braced himself against the impact. Next to her, Tepli muttered an oath and began to run, too slowly, toward the battle.

Beryl wanted to run away, but Arap Maina's danger tugged at her, like a rope tied around her waist. She followed Tepli, her eyes fixed on the solitary figure facing the lion's charge. When the lion was upon him, Arap Maina did not flinch. The great claws raked his shoulder, but he thrust his spear into the shoulder of the beast as he leapt. The lion roared in pain and fell to its uninjured side.

"Arap Maina!" Beryl cried, her heart pounding.

Hunter and lion rolled away from each other. Arap Maina's spear was lodged deep in the lion's shoulder, and blood flowed down its forelegs. Arap Maina came back to his feet. His blood turned his *shuka* a darker red. He and the lion circled each other warily. Arap Maina held only his knife now.

Beryl and Tepli were a dozen yards away. Tepli hesitated, his eyes judging how best to help Arap Maina.

Thinking only of distracting the lion, Beryl held her spear in front of her and rushed closer. "Eele! Eele!" she shouted.

The lion angrily shook his mane and turned his great head toward Beryl. His eyes were dilated from his battle with Arap Maina, but now they focused on her. She wasn't a warrior, she was prey. In an instant, the lion abandoned Arap Maina and went after Beryl.

Beryl froze. Her hands gripped her spear as tightly as though it were her only hope. The lion roared, and she could see his large teeth and a surprisingly pink tongue. The lion gathered himself to leap.

But Tepli was there. He swept Beryl away from the lion's path and then knelt in the dirt. As the beast passed over his head, Tepli used his spear to pierce its chest from underneath. Beryl curled up on the ground, trying to make herself small.

"Eele! Eele!" he shouted. "I am Tepli and I shall kill the lion!"

The lion was impaled on the spear, but still alive. From Beryl's vantage point on the ground, Tepli was terrible to watch. His neck muscles swelled like an angry snake. His mouth foamed with white flecks of rage. He was so brave! But the lion, even wounded, was still so very dangerous.

The beast whipped around and clawed Tepli's shoulder. Arap Maina appeared and started stabbing the lion's back with his knife. The lion's body heaved back and forth, knocking Tepli to the ground.

Terrified, Beryl saw that Tepli was not moving. Arap Maina kept stabbing. Finally, the lion's lifeblood pumped itself out and the great animal toppled over.

Beryl was trembling all over. She felt dampness between her legs, and realized she had wet herself. Her hand still gripped her spear, still unblooded. She pushed herself up off the ground and forced herself to move past the still lion and toward the warriors, who had placed themselves between her and danger. They lay in the dirt, bleeding freely into the grass.

"The dead don't bleed," she chanted. "The dead don't bleed."

Arap Maina's eyes were open. He grimaced in pain, panting hard.

"You're alive!" she cried.

"Of course," he said.

"What can I do?" she whispered.

"Get my spear," he replied.

Beryl nodded. She knew a *murani*'s weapon was a part of himself. Arap Maina's spear was still in the beast's shoulder, and its great head hung down over the weapon. She was relieved to see the lion was not still bleeding. She reached out, hardly daring to breathe, and touched its mane. It was rough and tangled to her fingertips. Gathering up her courage, she grabbed a hunk of mane and pulled. She had to use both hands to lift the heavy head away from the spear embedded deep in the lion's chest. She braced her bare foot against the soft hide for leverage to pull it out. It finally came loose with a horrible sucking noise.

She carefully wiped the steel blade on the grass and brought the spear to Arap Maina. He raised himself up, despite the bloody claw marks on his shoulder, and examined his weapon.

"Thank Enka that the blade is not chipped." He looked up at her, and she saw that his eyes were as clear as ever. "Now bring Tepli his spear."

Steeling herself, she returned to the lion. Tepli's spear was not so deeply stuck. She carried it to her reluctant bodyguard, who lay motionless on the ground. His chest was covered with crimson blood, his own and the lion's. She reached down gingerly to touch his arm. At that moment, his eyes flew open. She said nothing but she wanted to shout for joy.

"Beru," said Tepli in a faint voice. "You smell."

She almost laughed out loud with relief. "I know," she said. "I was afraid."

"You were a fool to come so close."

"I know." Beryl stared at the ground. "It was stupid. Please forgive me."

"But . . ." he went on. "It was something a warrior would do."

Beryl burst into tears of relief and gratitude. Tepli shook his head irritably at her weakness. Only then did he seem to notice the gashes on his chest. He prodded them with the tip of a finger and cursed. He saw his spear in Beryl's hands and reclaimed it with a scowl.

"Eele, eele!" The other warriors finally returned. Their faces fell when they saw the lion was already dead. Tepli told the others that the white girl had helped to fight the lion.

Later, the warriors cut off the lion's ears and paws. One *murani* came over to Arap Maina and shoved the ears onto the tip of his spear. Another warrior brought a paw to Tepli's spear, and two more brought a paw to push onto Beryl's small spear. The remaining warriors slit open the beast's belly and began to cut away its fat.

Beryl squatted beside Arap Maina, where he was resting against a tree trunk. "Arap Maina, what are they doing?"

"Lion's fat is good for our wounds. They will bring it to the tribe's healer."

Beryl glanced guiltily at Arap Maina's wounded shoulder. "I'm sorry I didn't obey you. I wanted to help."

"I know."

"I never meant for you or Tepli to be hurt!"

"Of course not. But let me tell you this. A warrior does not run from battle. As you did not run. The lion is dead. We are alive. A good day's hunt."

"But your shoulder . . . Tepli's chest."

"Beru, being bitten or clawed is no tragedy for a *murani*. Our scars are proof that we were in the battle. Ask the others—they wish they were in our place."

Beryl watched the men who had finished bandaging Tepli and were now skinning the lion. The warriors chanted in praise of the three who faced the lion, but there was envy in their singing.

"Beru, you did well," said Arap Maina.

"So today I am a *murani*?" she asked hopefully.

He laughed, and choosing his words carefully, he replied, "As much as a white girl can ever be a *murani*, you are one today."

Tired as she was, Beryl had no trouble keeping the slower pace the warriors set on the way home. As they walked, she dropped back to ask Arap Maina one last question.

"Why did you shout your name before you stabbed the lion?"

"It is the *murani* way. We claim the kill so no other warrior can take away the glory."

"But you were facing the lion alone. No one else could have claimed it."

"Beru, in that moment, between me and the lion, he needed to hear the name of the man who would kill him. And I needed to remember that I fought not only for myself, but for the honor of my tribe."

Clutching her lion's paw, Beryl repeated as if it were an oath, "I fought for the honor of my tribe."

I climb into the cockpit of <u>The Messenger</u>. She's a four-seater, built to be light and fast. But today she's weighted down with nineteen hundred pounds of fuel: tanks in the wings, in the center body, next to me, and behind me where the passenger seats should be. There's hardly room for my provisions and my maps.

I latch the door and look out down the long military runway. A civilian runway won't give me enough distance to get the heavy plane off the ground.

I call out, "Switches on. . . . Contact."

My mechanic swings the propeller.

After a heartbeat of silence, the engine roars to life. I push the throttle forward and the airplane hesitates. She's too heavy. <u>The Messenger</u> is rebellious and surly. Well, I've had more than one reluctant horse under me. I coax it forward. Sullenly, she yields to persuasion.

I won't circle on the runway: I dare not waste a drop of fuel. I head straight west. She goes faster and faster.

"Come on," I mutter. "Lift!"

And she does. Scant seconds before I run out of tarmac, the nose goes up and the tail drops. I just clear the trees, but what more do I need?

In my triumph, I shout, "Eele! Eele! Beryl!"

CHAPTER THIRTEEN

"WARTHOGS AREN'T VERY DANGEROUS," TEPLI SAID. "UNLESS THEY are cornered." Tepli, who was recovering well from his wounds, had consented to bring Beryl and Kibii hunting. Kibii was pleased enough that Beryl hoped he might soon forgive her for the lion hunt.

Beryl and Kibii craned their necks to see the particular warthog they had just cornered. It had backed into the cave on the side of the hill, so its sharp tusks were facing his attackers.

"We must lure him out," Tepli said.

"How?" Beryl asked.

"I know," shouted Kibii excitedly. "My father has told me. Beru, do you have any paper?"

She reached into the wide pockets of her khaki shorts and pulled out a note from her father regarding the care of his horses while he was away. Tepli directed them to stand on each side of the hole while he stood in front and crumpled the paper loudly.

"Why is he doing that?" whispered Beryl to Kibii from their position flanking the cave.

"It drives the beast crazy. My father says it is the only useful thing the white man has brought to Africa." His nostrils flared, a sign that he was embarrassed. "Oh, Beru, I'm sorry."

"Not to worry. He's probably right. I don't like the sound of composition paper either."

Sure enough, the warthog quivered with rage until it could bear the noise no longer and attacked. Beryl and Kibii were ready with their spears, behind and above the beast. They thrust their blades in the fold of skin behind its neck, killing it instantly.

As they returned home, Kibii and Beryl chattered happily. It had been a successful hunt; not as dangerous as going after a lion, but still exciting. As Green Hills Farm came into view, Beryl remembered what she had managed to forget during the hunt.

"Has Mehru forgiven me for going on the lion hunt?" she asked.

"Of course not."

"But you have . . . yes?"

Kibii didn't answer.

"Kibii, you know why I had to do it. I won't get another chance." She sighed. "Today was probably my last hunt."

"Why?" Kibii asked, almost in spite of himself.

"My father will be back any day now. Have you forgotten that he went to Nairobi to find me a governess?"

"A governess?" Cocking his head to one side, Kibii stumbled on the unfamiliar word. "What is that?"

"It's not a thing, it's a person." Beryl gave him a baleful look. "Only white children have them. A teacher who will lock me inside and make me learn to read and do my numbers."

Kibii focused on the essential problem. "If you are locked up with books, how will you train with me?"

"I won't be able to." Throwing her plaited hair over her shoulder, she dislodged a shower of dirt and bits of leaves. "I'll be strapped into a dress and tied to a desk!"

"Then I shall go hunting without you," Kibii said with a shrug. "It is what you would do."

They had reached the path to Kibii's village. He said farewell, and Beryl continued to her hut. She stopped dead at the door. At her feet lay a limp bundle of fur—a hare. She nudged it with a toe to turn it over. She drew a sharp, horrified breath.

The animal's eyes and tender skin around its nose had been gnawed away, chunk by chunk. The underside of the hare was covered with crawling black ants.

"*Siafu!*" she hissed. Beryl had seen many frightening things, but nothing scared her like the *siafu*. When she woke sweating in the night, her heart beating fast, it was because the ants had invaded her nightmares. The black warrior ants lived only to swarm over living creatures and eat away their soft spots. A small contingent, an advance guard perhaps, left the hare to march purposefully toward Beryl's bare foot. She jumped up and down to scare them.

"Ah, *siafu*." A deep voice startled her. It was Arap Maina, looking down at the hare. He used a pitchfork to spear the carcass and toss it onto a heap of rubbish for burning.

"I hate them!" Beryl said, struggling to keep her voice even.

"Beru, answer me this. What does it mean when you see *siafu*?"

"Are they a bad omen?" The Nandi saw omens in everything.

Arap Maina shook his head with a small smile. "On the contrary; *siafu* mean the rains are coming. But if it is an omen you want, your father has come back safely."

As Beryl ran to the main house, she wondered briefly why Arap Maina had been smiling. But the thought was quickly replaced by the more important question: What would the governess be like? In her usual headlong rush, she plunged into the living room.

"Daddy!" she said breathlessly. "When did you . . . " Her voice trailed off as she saw what he held in his hands.

He was examining the skinned head of a lion. The rest of its fur was spread across his desk. The lion's noble brow mocked her, despite its missing ears.

"Why would Arap Maina give me this valuable skin?" the Captain asked grimly.

Beryl held out her hands and shrugged.

The Captain didn't need her to answer. "'A remembrance of Beryl's first lion hunt,' Arap Maina said. He expected me to be pleased. In fact, he expected me to know all about it."

He waited, impatient with her silence. Finally, he banged his fist on the desk. Even muffled by the lion skin, the sound threatened worse to come. "What do you have to say for yourself?" His voice was sharp, like a commander on the parade field.

"You said I could train with the Nandi, Daddy," she said, locking her knees to keep them from trembling.

"Did I say you could go kill a lion?" he shouted.

Taking a deep breath, she said, "I didn't actually kill that lion, Daddy."

"Beryl Clutterbuck, I didn't think you did. And you knew perfectly well that I never would have allowed you to go lion hunting."

"I knew if you brought back a governess, I might never get another chance. So I asked Arap Maina, and he let me go."

The Captain pinched the bridge of his nose. "Emma was right," he muttered. To Beryl, he said, "Don't you realize that you could have been maimed or even killed?"

"But I wasn't, Daddy. Arap Maina said I did well!"

"He told me that, too."

Beryl breathed easier; the pride in her father's voice was impossible to miss.

"He said I was brave to rush in after he had been hurt." His attention quickened, and she realized she had misstepped.

"Arap Maina was hurt? Protecting you?" He fixed her with a steely glance. "And now I'll pay for that, because he won't be able to work on the farm."

"He wasn't hurt badly. He didn't even cry."

"Of course he didn't, Beryl." The Captain looked down at the hide on his desk, his hand absently stroking the rough fur. "The Nandi train from boyhood to not react to pain. It's part of their rituals."

Beryl jumped in, eager to show her father how much she had learned. "I know all about it. The boy gets soaked with cold water. Then the boy's family chants, you know, to encourage him. They shout things like 'Don't flinch!,' 'Don't be a coward!,' and 'Make the cut sharp.' Then the *ol-oboini*, he's the elder, takes a sharp knife and cuts the boy . . . down there." Beryl gestured to below her father's waist. He pinched his nose harder, but his mouth twitched with laughter.

"Clutt!" Beryl looked up to see Emma standing in the doorway, her hands on Arthur's shoulders. Arthur's eyes were wide as saucers, and his hands were pulling at his trousers. Emma's face was pale. In a tight voice, she asked, "How in God's name can you let her know such things?"

"Daddy, I've never seen the ceremony," she assured him. "Girls aren't allowed."

Emma ignored Beryl, speaking only to the Captain. "What will Miss Le May think?"

Only then did Beryl see the stranger hovering behind Emma and Arthur. She was tall and broad-shouldered, with red hair and freckles. She wore a starched white cotton dress, now limp in the afternoon heat, and laced-up boots like Emma's. But her pock-marked face wasn't nearly as pretty as Emma's.

Beryl felt like a gazelle at the watering hole once a predator has come. Every instinct screamed, "Run!"

Flustered, Emma performed the introductions. "Beryl, this is Miss Le May. She will be your teacher."

"How do you do?" Miss Le May's voice was very proper. She said "How" very deliberately, as though she had to concentrate.

Beryl looked down at the floor and said nothing. Sighing, the Captain abandoned the lion skin and moved behind Beryl. He pressed his strong fingers into her shoulder blades.

"Howdoyoudo?" she mumbled, trying not to wince at his painful squeeze.

The Captain pulled out his watch to check the time. "Excellent," he pronounced, as he turned to leave the room. "Now I can concentrate on getting my mills up and running."

Running away is more like it, Beryl thought. From Emma's sour expression, Beryl suspected that she was thinking the same thing.

My little <u>Messenger</u> stinks of petrol. Eight thousand feet above the sea, tossed about by the North Atlantic winds, I wonder what makes me think this tin box can make it across the wide ocean. I think back to all those hours poring over blueprints and calculations. My engineers say the plane will fly because the mathematics prove it.

When I was a child, my father hired a governess to teach me arithmetic and multiplication. I didn't see the point. I've always trusted my instincts over the mathematics. I'll fly, not because of numbers scribbled on a piece of paper, but because I think I can.

CHAPTER FOURTEEN

CLASSES STARTED THE NEXT MORNING IN THE MAIN ROOM OF the Captain's house. The atmosphere resembled the stillness before a storm. Captain Clutterbuck was out on the farm. Emma and Arthur also made themselves scarce.

Miss Le May placed a stack of yellow books on the table. "I'm prepared for my duties," she began brightly. "I've brought the Crown Readers, the *Fundamentals of English Grammar*, and *Exercises in Practical Arithmetic*. I've been told they're the correct texts."

"I thought you were supposed to be a teacher?" Beryl asked suspiciously.

Miss Le May pinched her full lips together. "I can read and write—apparently that's more than you can do. Each morning we will do reading, and in the afternoon mathematics."

Narrowing her eyes, Beryl said, "Early mornings won't work. My father needs me to ride out every morning at six."

"Where are you riding out to? What about your schooling?"

"Riding out means to exercise the horses," Beryl explained in a scornful voice. "They're racing horses—not just anyone can ride them."

"You can come here after you've finished." Miss Le May's smile was not quite as bright. "I can see we both have a lot to learn from each other."

"I doubt it," said Beryl under her breath.

Miss Le May went on, "We will start with the alphabet. A, B, C, D . . ."

"E, F, G, H, I, J, K, L, M, N, O, P, Q, R, S, T, U, V, W, X, Y, Zed." Beryl rattled off the rest of the alphabet in one breath. She had the satisfaction of seeing the surprise on Miss Le May's face.

"Your mother said that . . ."

"She's not my mother!" Beryl interrupted. "She's not married to my father, and she never will be."

Miss Le May cleared her throat nervously. "Emma, then. She led me to believe that you knew nothing."

"Maybe it's Emma who doesn't know nothing," Beryl said crudely.

"Emma doesn't know *anything*," Miss Le May corrected.

Beryl giggled. Miss Le May didn't see what was funny.

"Does that mean you can read, too?" Miss Le May had an eager look on her face.

Beryl shrugged.

"Read this aloud." Miss Le May shoved one of her Crown Readers at Beryl.

Beryl looked down at the book, which must have been several

decades old. It was about small children getting a white puppy with a black spot over his eye. They called him Patches.

She tossed it aside. "Not likely. My father taught me to read much more interesting things." She ran over to her father's shelf, suspended midway up the wall. She pulled out a leather-bound book and carried it with reverence to lay it on the table.

Miss Le May glanced curiously at the book. "A Bible?" There was cautious approval in her voice.

"Why would I read a Bible?" Beryl asked. She opened the scrapbook filled with newspaper clippings. There was only one subject: Captain Clutterbuck. The most recent page blazed a headline: "Clutt Takes Home the Prize." There was a striking picture of the Captain astride The Baron. Both Beryl and Miss Le May stared at the photograph.

"He's a handsome man, your father," Miss Le May said with a smile, her tongue darting across her lips.

"I suppose," Beryl said acidly.

Miss Le May considered the primer and the leather book. There was no doubt which was more interesting. "Well, as you have already started with these ..."

That was the morning's lesson in reading. The afternoon's mathematics lesson was not so smooth. From the moment it began, the battle lines were drawn.

"Beryl, if five plus five equals ten, then what does five plus six equal?"

"Why would I care?"

"Even your precious Nandi warriors must count their cattle." Miss Le May's voice sounded stretched, as though it might snap.

"When you know each animal's name, you don't need to count."

"Well, *you* do. Your father has too many 'orses, I mean horses, not to count them."

"I know all the names of Daddy's horses. That's important, not stupid numbers."

"Beryl, I will not tolerate disrespect in this 'ouse. I mean house."

A suspicion took root in Beryl's mind. To test her theory, she asked, "Don't you 'ate 'orrible girls who ride 'orrid 'orses?"

Miss Le May stood up and paced around the room like a caged animal. She took a deep breath and came back to stand in front of Beryl.

"Beryl, this is your last chance to cooperate."

"Or else you'll 'it me?"

Miss Le May reached into her skirt's deep pocket and brought out a heavy wooden ruler. "Let's try one last time, shall we? Five plus six?"

Beryl stared at the ruler. Her father had smacked her once or twice, but no one else had ever struck her. Miss Le May wouldn't dare.... Her heart pounded and her breathing grew shallow. "I don't care," she whispered.

Faster than Beryl could pull her hands back, Miss Le May brought the ruler down hard on Beryl's fingers.

Thwap!

At first Beryl was too stunned and shocked to react. Her eyes watered for a moment, but she blinked the tears back.

Miss Le May stood still, her pale eyes wide and a dreadful smile on her lips. Beryl swallowed hard and braced herself.

"Five plus six?"

"I don't care."

Thwap!

After half an hour, Miss Le May was exhausted and Beryl's knuckles were cut and bleeding. But Beryl didn't cry out, not once. Arap Maina would be proud.

Arthur poked his head in to see what was happening. His eyes widened, but Beryl jerked her head toward the stables where Kibii was working. He got her message, and darted away before Miss Le May noticed him.

A few minutes later, Beryl saw Kibii's head appear at the window. He beckoned to her. Beryl nodded imperceptibly.

"Miss Le May, I think my father is returning." She was gratified to see the blood run out of the governess's face.

Miss Le May quickly put away the ruler and went to the door. Beryl was only waiting for her chance. The moment the governess's back was turned, Beryl ran toward the window. With a leap, she was halfway over the sill. Kibii was there to grab her arms and pull her out. In an instant they were halfway across the yard, running hard.

Realizing she had been tricked, Miss Le May came running after them. She galumphed like a plow horse.

"Camiscan," Beryl said to Kibii. They darted into Camiscan's stall. Speaking calming words and patting his muzzle reassuringly, they stood with their backs against the wall and waited.

"Beryl! Beryl! Where are you?" They could hear Miss Le May shouting. Finally the redheaded teacher looked over the half door.

"There you are, you little brat. Get out 'ere right now. We are still doing arithmetic."

"Come and get me," said Beryl.

"Fine. I will." Miss Le May pulled open the stall door and strode in. She knew nothing about horses, not even enough to be afraid. Camiscan whinnied in warning and pawed the ground dangerously. Miss Le May screamed. The stallion reared as high as he could in his stall, his lips curled back from his teeth. Too terrified to move, Miss Le May stood screaming in the doorway. A stable lad rushed up and pulled her to safety, slamming the stall door shut.

"Get your filthy black hands off me," Miss Le May snapped at the boy.

"Ungrateful," Beryl whispered to Kibii in Swahili.

The governess smoothed her hair and rearranged her dress. "Beryl Clutterbuck, this isn't finished. If you want war, you'll get war." As she turned, her foot slipped in a pile of manure. Beryl and Kibii howled with laughter, avoiding Camiscan's hooves as he moved uneasily in his stall. Miss Le May wiped her boot clean and stalked away.

When Kibii finally stopped laughing, he turned suddenly solemn. "War?"

"*Kita.*"

"Oh. That is not good."

"No, it's not," she said. "Look." She proudly held out her bloody fingers for Kibii's inspection.

"I know. Arthur told me. It was good that you did not cry. But she liked hurting you too much."

"Thank you for helping me to escape. Luckily, Daddy doesn't have glass in the windows yet." Beryl flexed her fingers painfully. "She's a witch, isn't she?"

"With that red hair, it would not surprise me if she was a devil." Kibii was only half joking.

"Perhaps she is."

"You should tell your father," Kibii said.

"Would you ask your father for help if Mehru bullied you?"

A wry smile appeared on his lips. "I would not need help with Mehru. He is a coward."

"So is she." She punched one hand into her palm and winced. "This fight is between her and me."

I'm surrounded by a wall of fuel inside my little Messenger. I've no gauges, no way to know how much petrol I have. The tank sitting next me has a happy little sign: "This tank good for four hours." But at what airspeed? What about the headwinds pushing me back, using up my precious fuel? When the main tank is through, I have to turn a valve to open the next one. I dare not waste a drop. So the trick is to wait until the engine stops completely before I switch tanks. I'm dreading that moment.

I open the window to get some relief from the smell of petrol. The driving rain spatters my face like buckshot. I pull out my chart of the Atlantic and a gust of wind blows it out of my hand. I see it floating down to the cold, dark ocean. Ah, well—there's nothing on that chart but water. I almost want to turn back, but of course I can't do that.

As a child, I learned you never give up. Never.

CHAPTER FIFTEEN

IT WAS A STALEMATE UNTIL THE CAPTAIN AND EMMA WENT away to the horse sales in Nairobi a week later. The rainy season was beginning; the Captain could be spared from the farm. Emma decided to bring Arthur, but insisted that Beryl should not miss any schooling. Arap Maina had taken the boys to help him bring new cattle to the village. Beryl and Miss Le May were alone.

Beryl saw that the rules had changed as soon as she sat down at the table that afternoon. Even the room looked different. Although it was the middle of the day, the room was lit with a paraffin lantern. A table was pulled across the doorway to the hall. Emma's new lacy curtains were drawn across the windows and tied down. Worst of all, Miss Le May looked pleased.

Beryl stared down at the bruises and half-healed cuts on her fingers. Her father and Emma hadn't even noticed her injuries before they left.

"So, Beryl Clutterbuck," Miss Le May said. "We are on our own for a fortnight."

"Lovely," Beryl muttered.

"Don't mumble, dear. Let's take out our notebook, shall we?" Miss Le May stood over Beryl, looking down at her.

Beryl opened her notebook, but didn't pick up her pencil.

"Six plus six?" Miss Le May said sweetly.

"I don't know," Beryl answered.

With a smile as broad as her freckled forehead, Miss Le May asked, "And you don't care?"

"No," Beryl said warily.

Miss Le May gave a deep, theatrical sigh and said in a sad voice, "I was so afraid you would say that, my dear." She walked over to the door and bolted it shut.

Beryl's stomach contracted into a tight ball.

"Beryl, you're so fond of the natives, I thought I would adopt one of their methods." She reached into her satchel and pulled out a *kiboko*. "I'm told this is made from rhino hide. Your precious Nandi use it to discipline cattle."

Beryl glowered from under her eyebrows. "Are you calling me a cow?"

"No, my dear. Just a discipline problem." And with that, Miss Le May flicked the whip, cracking it across the room.

Beryl straightened up, her eyes darting around the room, looking for any way out. But Miss Le May had planned too carefully.

"Six plus six?"

"I don't care."

Crack!

The whip slashed across Beryl's back. For an instant, the pain knocked the breath out of her. She bit down on her lip to keep any sound from escaping.

Miss Le May repeated her question.

Through her clenched jaw, Beryl muttered, "I don't care."

Crack!

Under her breath, Beryl repeated over and over, "Don't flinch. Don't be a coward. Don't flinch." The Nandi ritual helped a little. The pain receded a tiny bit. She sneaked a glance at Miss Le May. Her eyes were unfocused, and her mouth was parted as she panted with the effort of beating Beryl.

"Six plus six?"

After a moment, there was another crack.

Shuddering with waves of pain, Beryl deliberately closed her mouth tightly and refused to speak a word.

"Answer me!"

Beryl almost smiled at the desperation in Miss Le May's voice.

"If you won't talk, I'll . . . I'll . . ." The governess trailed off as she realized that Beryl had withstood her worst. She paced wildly about the room until she had an idea. She grabbed Beryl by the arm and dragged her to the door. Unbolting it, she checked to see that there were no servants around. Then she pulled Beryl to the *rondavel* and threw her onto the hard cow-dung floor.

"You can stay there until you find your voice, young lady. We'll see 'ow long you last without food or water. There won't be any natives or 'orses to help you this time."

She shoved the door shut and barred it with a block of wood. Beryl's windows had shutters, which she rarely used, but now Miss

Le May slammed them closed and pulled the bar to lock them from the outside. Beryl could hear her stomping away.

Huddled on the floor, Beryl tried not to think how much her back hurt. She reached behind her and fingered the tatters of her linen shirt.

"I hate her. I hate her. I hate her," she chanted, her words throbbing in time with the slashes across her shoulders. "I wish she would fall into a pit filled with *siafu*."

She remembered the dead hare and the ants marching toward her hut. In the dim light, she imagined the tramping of thousands of insect feet homing in on her blood-soaked back. She scrambled up on her bed and huddled under her blanket and finally gave way to the sobs she had held back since the first crack of the whip. She called for her father, for Kibii, for Arap Maina. Even Emma would offer a gentle hand on her aching back. Her tears exhausted, she finally fell asleep.

She awoke to the thunder of rain on her thatch roof. Through the gaps in the shutters' slats, she could see twilight had fallen. It was still raining. The hunger in her belly was a distraction to the stinging of her back. She had missed lunch and dinner.

"I won't stay here like a prisoner," she announced to the empty room. Swinging her feet to the floor, she winced at the burning in her back and shoulders. She shoved against the door, but Miss Le May had blocked it well. The window, too. Beryl lit her paraffin lantern and looked around her hut at every wall, every crack. She was used to thinking of it as a refuge, not as a prison.

She held the lantern up and noticed a wet stain on the back wall near the corner. The wall was buckling from the rain, and a narrow crack had appeared in the hardened mud. She pulled out her knife and began scraping frantically. After what seemed like hours, the crack was bigger; big enough to let the rain pour in, but not quite big enough to let Beryl escape.

She dug through her belongings under the bed and found her elephant tusk. Using its sharp end, she dug into the dampened wall. The warm rain made the ivory slippery in her muddy hands. Finally, the crack was big enough for her thin body. She forced herself through, sparing her back as well as she could. Outside, the water felt cool on her bare skin, soothing the smarting cuts.

A sound behind her alerted her that she wasn't alone. It was Buller. The poor old dog was waiting for her. She fondled his ears.

"Hey, boy. Want to come with me? I could use the company."

Although Buller had recovered from his injuries, he had never been the same after the leopard attack. These days he preferred to sit on the porch and watch life on the farm. With a whimper, he pressed his nose against her hand, then went to lie under the thatch hanging off her hut.

"Fair-weather friend," Beryl muttered. Without a backward glance, she ran into the forest. Its nighttime noises were stilled by the cool rain. She needed to find shelter before nightfall. She considered going to the Nandi, but then shook her head. "It's the first place she'll look," she said to herself.

Then Beryl remembered the day she hunted warthog. The warthog's hole would be empty now. She began running toward the meadow where they had hunted. The hole was still there, a narrow slit in the hill. She found a long stick and poked it through the entrance. The last thing she needed today was another battle.

The cave seemed empty. Streaming with water, her bare feet covered with mud, Beryl gratefully crawled backward into the warthog's hole.

Beryl lived rough for another two days, eating roots and berries. On the third night, worried that her cuts might get infected, she went to the Nandi village. She arrived at sunset, to be greeted by the tribe's pack of dogs. She walked straight to Arap Maina's hut.

"Beru! Where have you been? We have been worried. Come in and have something to eat." Naipende was as welcoming as Beryl could have hoped. She would never admit it, but she had been lonely in her exile.

She slipped off her filthy shirt and turned her back to Kibii's mother. Naipende's sharply indrawn breath told Beryl that the wounds were as ugly as they felt. "Your father will not like this, Beru," she said as she hurried off to find a balm made from tree sap to coat the welts.

"No, he won't," Beryl said with satisfaction.

Beryl stayed with the Nandi for almost two weeks. Her friends reported that Miss Le May was frantic with worry. She wasn't sleeping, and even her hearty appetite had been affected. The governess couldn't understand why no one was concerned. But the servants, who knew exactly where Beryl was, thought it was a good joke.

The day before her father was due to return, Beryl went back and reported for her reading lesson as though nothing had happened.

"Where 'ave you been?" Miss Le May was flabbergasted. "We thought a lion 'ad eaten you. Wait until I tell your father."

Beryl drew herself up tall until her eyes were on level with Miss Le May's freckled, pitted face. "Tell him what? That you beat me so badly I bled? That you locked me in my hut? That I escaped in fear for my life? That I have been missing for two weeks? What do you think my father will say?"

Without a word, Miss Le May pulled out the leather book of clippings.

A week passed before Miss Le May dared to bring up mathematics again. Beryl had not said a word to her father, so the governess must have felt safe.

"Five plus seven?"

"You know I don't care."

"Beryl, that's enough. I've still got my ruler."

Beryl looked out the window. Her father was returning home, no doubt for a cup of tea. She calculated how long it would take him to reach the house.

"I'm not afraid of your ruler," she said. "Or your whip." She stuck out her tongue.

As Beryl knew she would, Miss Le May pulled out the familiar wooden ruler and held it over Beryl's hand.

"Five plus seven?" Miss Le May asked.

"I don't care."

Thwap!

"Ahh!" Beryl howled in pain. "That hurt. Ow! Ow! Daddy!" And she burst into tears that would make a crocodile proud.

Captain Clutterbuck rushed into the room. With a glance, he took in the situation. In an icy voice, he said, "Miss Le May, exactly what do you think you are doing?"

The scene was everything Beryl could have wished for. The

Captain raged. Miss Le May was sullen and afraid. Emma tried to defend the governess, but even she was appalled by the marks on Beryl's hands and back. Within two hours, Miss Le May's bags were packed and she was mounted on a slow pony for the five-mile trip to Nakuru. As she left the farm, Beryl appeared at the edge of the forest to say her farewell.

"Hey, Miss Le May! Five plus seven is twelve. Thank you for teaching me!"

With a look of loathing on her pitted face, Miss Le May rode away from Green Hills farm. Her back was slumped in humiliation. Beryl waved until she was out of sight.

LOCATION: Somewhere over the North Atlantic

DATE: 02:00 A.M. GMT, 5 September, 1936

I wouldn't have imagined that there was an expanse of desolation so big in the whole world as the waste of sky and water between England and North America. When I climb, I get sleet. When I drop, rain. If I skim the sea, I'm surrounded by fog. I can't see a thing beyond my wingtips. I'm afraid I'll go crazy.

I have to remind myself what Tom and all the other long-distance flyers say—the worst part of these flights is sheer loneliness.

The night cannot last forever. The winds seem to have forgiven me for whatever sins I might have committed. I shake myself for being so silly. I've overcome greater obstacles than this. I can't imagine that I won't make it.

←--→

CHAPTER SIXTEEN

TAP TAP TAP.

Emma, seated at the head of the table, was playing the Captain's hostess. The rough table was covered with fine linen and china she had imported from England. The men, new settlers visiting the Clutterbuck farm, were dining on roast gazelle and drinking port.

Tap tap tap.

Trying to place the odd sound, Emma glanced first toward Beryl. Beryl was jiggling her feet and tapping her fork against the table.

"Stop fidgeting this instant," Emma hissed.

"I'm finished with lunch—may I be excused?" Beryl's request came out in a rush.

Emma glanced down the table to the Captain, who was completely engrossed in a story he was telling. She sighed. "Very well."

As though Beryl were a tightly wound spring, she bounced up and ran out of the room. Scant seconds later, she was outside, heaving in deep breaths of fresh air, wishing the intruders would go away. For once, the problem was not Emma. Lord Delamere, her father's patron, had brought the newcomers to the farm. He was a close friend of the family and of Beryl's, but she couldn't stand the others. For two days, the pink-faced men had monopolized her father's time, mopping their brows, smoking their cigars, drinking the Captain's precious whiskey, and examining claims on a map.

Once safely in her own hut, she pulled off the scratchy muslin dress Emma had insisted she wear and replaced it with a dirty scarlet *shuka* draped over her shoulder and knotted under one arm. Moments later, she was running down the hill to the Nandi village.

The sound of her feet kept an even rhythm on the narrow path. Arap Maina's words rumbled in her head: "Muffle your steps; imagine you have wings on your ankles." Perhaps if Beryl hadn't been concentrating so hard on her feet, she would have seen the predator waiting for her behind the stand of cedar trees. Instead, she was taken unawares by the dark streak of muscle with a slash of red. It rushed out of hiding to tackle her low around the knees.

She fell face first to the ground with an impact that stole her breath. Her attacker gained his feet and tried to put a heel in her back. But Beryl had not trained tirelessly with Kibii for nothing. In a single movement she had pulled out her knife and flipped over.

"Mehru," she gasped. Her heartbeat sped up as she saw his long knife. His smile was full of the bad blood between them. Mehru's name meant "tall," and he towered over Beryl lying in the dirt, blocking her sun. He brandished his knife with the ease of long practice.

"So, Beru, when Arap Maina is not here to protect you, you grovel in the dirt like a dog," he taunted her in Swahili.

"Mehru, is that your father's weapon? I know you haven't earned your own yet," she taunted back.

His face grew even darker with anger. He tilted his head back to let out the Nandi battle yell. In the instant that his eyes were skyward, Beryl wriggled out of harm's way. Mehru plunged down with his knife, but Beryl was no longer there. She leapt to her feet and faced him, warrior to warrior. She shouted her own battle cry, her lip twisted in her best fighting snarl.

Mehru went after her, jabbing with his knife. Beryl swiftly moved back. He ran toward her, cutting and slashing. His blade caught her thigh. Blood spurted. He laughed.

Panting, Beryl pushed against the cut with her palm. It wasn't serious, she decided. She moved in with her own knife and caught the fleshy part of his arm with the point of her blade. She thrust again, trying to keep him off balance.

"Were you afraid to challenge me in the open?" she asked, dodging his longer reach.

They heard footsteps running up the path and they both turned their heads a fraction to see who was coming. It was Kibii.

"Enough!" Kibii ordered, sounding as authoritative as his father. "You have each drawn blood. This should be settled with bare hands." Kibii flashed Mehru a vindictive grin. "That is, if you dare. Beru is very good at wrestling."

Both Beryl and Mehru were breathing hard, covered with sweat. Their wounds bled freely. Not taking their eyes from each other, they let their knives fall. Holding up their empty hands, they moved toward each other. By Nandi tradition, the first to bring the other to the ground would be the winner. Kibii watched in silence.

Mehru tried to use his greater height to overpower Beryl, but she was ready. She hooked a foot around his leg and jerked. He nearly fell, but saved himself by grabbing her *shuka* to pull himself upright. The fabric tore from her body. She kneed him hard in the groin. He grunted and bent over for a split second.

Instantly, Beryl looped one arm over his neck to keep his head down. She dropped her body under his and wedged her shoulder against his chest. She bent her knees and pushed with all her power at his chest, while pulling down his head. Just as she hoped, his body flew up, feet first, into the air, and he sailed over her shoulder to fall to the hard, dry ground. Even winded, on his back in the dust, Mehru still tried to pull her down with him. But her thigh was slippery with blood and he lost his grip.

She knelt on his chest, gave a crow of victory, and clasped her hands above her head. His height and his surprise tactics had not been enough. She had won. Kibii whooped for her. Mehru would never live down being beaten by a girl—and an English girl, at that.

"Beryl Clutterbuck!" A voice sharp as Mehru's blade cut through their cheers.

Beryl turned to see her father standing on the path, his face pale. Behind him, Lord Delamere and some of the other strangers stared with their mouths hanging open.

"Daddy!" Beryl said. She stared as her father strode over, tearing off his shirt. He grabbed her arm and roughly pulled her away from Mehru.

"Daddy, you're hurting me," Beryl protested.

"Shut up, Beryl!" The Captain wrapped his shirt around her. Beryl realized that she was naked except for her underwear and she was covered with blood, her own and Mehru's. Her father spun her around and pushed her toward Lord Delamere, whose normally cheerful face was grave. "Delamere, for God's sake, take her up to the house."

"Clutt, what are you going to do?" asked Delamere, clasping Beryl to his chest. Despite the damp heat of the afternoon, Beryl shivered at the chill in his voice.

"He interfered with my daughter. I'm going to kill the bastard," the Captain said, reaching for the holster under his arm.

"No, Daddy!" shrieked Beryl. "You don't understand. Mehru challenged me! I won! It's over."

But her words were smothered against Delamere's chest. Kibii had seen enough; he turned and raced away down the hill toward the village.

Delamere thrust Beryl behind him and moved to intercept the Captain. He laid a large, gnarled hand on his friend's shoulder and spoke to him in low, urgent tones. "Clutt, murder is no answer. We'll place him in charge with the authorities. He'll hang for certain."

Beryl stood, trembling in the too-large shirt. This game had become something much more deadly. She prayed her father would see reason. Finally, he handed Lord Delamere his pistol. She exhaled in sharp relief.

Mehru cowered on the ground. Although he spoke no English, he understood guns. His body relaxed when he saw Lord Delamere pocket the pistol. So he was unprepared when the Captain rushed in and kicked him hard. His booted foot swung back again and again. Wincing but not crying out, Mehru curled up and tried to ride the blows.

"Daddy, stop! He didn't do anything!" Beryl screamed.

He ignored her. She tried to move forward, but Lord Delamere held her back.

"Lord D," she begged. "Please make him stop!" He ignored her, as did the other men. They watched, grim-faced and silent, as the Captain tried to kick Mehru to death.

Tears ran down Beryl's cheeks, and it seemed like forever before she saw Arap Maina running toward them with half a dozen angry young warriors. They had had no time to paint their faces for battle, but they had their spears. They were magnificent. Beryl wished she were standing with them instead of with these fat white men.

"Sahib, please stop beating this boy," Arap Maina said in a loud, but respectful voice. Behind him the warriors growled. His authority was barely keeping them in check.

With the exception of Beryl, Captain Clutterbuck, and Lord Delamere, the settlers did not understand Arap Maina's Swahili. They moved their hands to their weapons. Beryl's heart pumped more loudly than it had during the fight.

The Captain kicked Mehru's body again. "Stay out of this, Arap Maina." He didn't seem to notice the armed warriors. "You don't know what he did." His heel caught Mehru's head.

"With all respect, sahib, you do not know, either." Arap Maina's voice was calm but urgent. It sliced through the Captain's rage like a machete.

"I know what I see. This boy cut my daughter, pulled away her clothing . . ." The Captain couldn't finish his sentence, but he stopped kicking.

With a slight smile that did not reach his worried eyes, Arap

Maina said, "I disagree. I see a fight. A foolish boy tried to surprise Beru. But she was too swift for him. He cut her with his knife, but she cut him with hers."

The Captain seized on his words. "So he did attack her."

"As a warrior stalks another warrior, sahib. An honorable challenge."

"He cut her." The Captain spoke slowly, as though Arap Maina were an idiot.

"They cut each other. And then, as is our custom, each having drawn blood, they went to hand combat. And, as you see, Beru was the winner."

On the ground, Mehru did not move. His eyes were closed. Beryl prayed he wasn't dead.

Arap Maina sensed the dangerous wind was shifting. He pursued his good beginning. "Cluttabucki, you know your daughter is part of our tribe. No one would hurt her."

The Captain looked over to Beryl. She silently begged him to listen to reason. As suddenly as it had come, the fury left the Captain's body. His thick neck relaxed. He dragged the back of his hand across his sopping forehead.

Beryl, straining to hear, thought her father whispered, "What have I done? I might have killed this boy. . . . What am I to do with her?" The Captain turned his back on Arap Maina, an old friend who was now almost an enemy, and stared blankly at his daughter.

Beryl broke free from Lord Delamere and lurched away into the forest. Her leg was still bleeding, but her body was decently covered by her father's shirt.

The darkness goes on forever, and I'm flying blind.

I pull my compass from its pocket in the door. Tom gave it to me long ago, in Africa. He said, "Trust this, but nothing else. When you're up there, instruments can go wrong. If you can't fly without looking at your airspeed and your altimeter—well, then, you can't fly. You're like somebody who only knows what he thinks after reading the newspaper. The compass will tell you where you ought to be going—and the rest is up to you."

My compass tells me my heading is correct. I have to trust it. Once or twice the moon has made a brief appearance, but there are no landmarks to check my course. There's nothing but water.

An electrical storm pops up, just to make things more interesting. The sorry thing is that I welcome the storm—at least I can see something besides clouds and water. I'm flying at two thousand feet. I'd rather fly lower, to keep my eye on the ocean, but the wind is bucking like a wild stallion. Too dangerous.

A huge gust of wind grabs my little plane and shakes it. <u>The Messenger</u> takes a terrific toss. Something's wrong; I can't imagine why the gauges are fluctuating so wildly. Think, Beryl, think: Why is the plane behaving in such an extraordinary manner? A flash of lightning outside. Where's the water?

I look up. The water is above my head. I'm flying upside down. I've never felt so disoriented.

CHAPTER SEVENTEEN

EVERYTHING HAD CHANGED. UNTIL THAT AFTERNOON, BERYL HAD moved easily between her father's world and the Nandi village. But on the path that afternoon, with the thuds of the Captain's boot against Mehru's skull, she had seen that the divide was as big as the Great Rift Valley.

Night had fallen completely before Beryl could bring herself to leave the protection of the forest. She came up the path slowly, past the edge of the stables. She stopped to greet Camiscan in his darkened stall. He neighed, first in warning and then in recognition.

"Here, boy," she said, holding out her hand. The stallion whinnied gently and nuzzled her palm, tasting for the treat she usually brought him.

"Not tonight, boy. I have to go home and get some sleep. Tomorrow, I'll bring you something sweet." She stroked his muzzle and gave him a small kiss.

"Coo-ee, I can't believe you kiss him, Beryl. He bites everybody!"

It was Arthur, out hours past his bedtime. He was in his nightshirt, and he looked up at her through his tangled dark curls. "Are you in trouble, Beryl?"

"What have you heard?" she asked.

"Everybody's upset, but no one will tell me why." He took the last few steps separating them and touched her arm. "You'll tell me, right?"

"I would, if I knew myself." She hugged him. His head barely reached her chest, but his sturdy embrace made her feel better. "Come on, let me take you to the house before Emma has a fit."

Arthur put a trusting hand in hers and they walked to the large cedar house. She could smell the fire burning, and the glow at the windows beckoned her. She shooed Arthur in the side door and walked away toward her own hut. Slipping inside, she sighed in relief. She lit her lamp with one of her carefully guarded store of safety matches.

Beryl flopped down on her bed and examined the wound on her thigh. The bleeding was long stopped, but it needed some first aid. Wondering if she could pilfer a bandage from the main house without meeting her father, she was startled by a gentle tap on the door.

"Come in," she said after a brief moment.

The door opened and a woman holding a lamp stepped in.

"Emma," Beryl said coldly. At least it wasn't her father.

"Beryl," Emma responded. Her voice had no warmth either. A basket hung over her arm, and she brought it to Beryl's bed. "I brought my medical kit." She pulled out white gauze and a bottle of iodine. There was no table, so she dragged over an empty crate and laid out her supplies.

"How did you know I was back?" Beryl asked as she looked warily at the iodine.

"Beryl, you don't think Arthur can leave the house in the middle of the night without my knowing? It was his idea to wait in the stables."

"That little sneak. He didn't tell me."

"You aren't the only one who has secrets." Emma laid out a clean nightdress, the kind Beryl never bothered to wear. "Pull off that filthy shirt."

The Captain's shirt was stained with blood and dirt from the forest. It wasn't worth an infection just to irritate Emma. Beryl pulled off the shirt.

Emma touched the barely healed scars on Beryl's back and sighed. "Let's get you in the bath."

"I don't have a bath."

Emma held up the lamp to illuminate the darkest part of the hut. She pointed to a canvas bathtub that had not been there in the morning. Beryl walked over to it and saw that it was half full of tepid water. She looked at Emma suspiciously.

"It's high time you had a proper bathtub," Emma said. "Get in. We can't bandage that wound until you are clean."

Beryl stepped gingerly into the tub. She winced when the water touched her wound. Without a word, Emma handed her a cloth and a bar of soap. Beryl began to wash herself while Emma pulled out more wonders from her basket.

"I've brought you some dinner. I can't believe that you *like* eating roots, or whatever you find out there. There's cold meat and some cheese and fruit."

Beryl couldn't think of anything to say except "Thank you."

Emma sat on a wooden box next to the tub. "Beryl, a talk between us is long overdue."

Beryl slipped under the water. She held her breath as long as she could, but when she surfaced and opened her eyes, Emma was still there.

"Your father was very upset today," began Emma.

"I know. But he didn't understand. If he had only asked me . . ."

"Beryl, what do you expect? He saw you without your clothes, bleeding, and being attacked by a . . . a . . . savage black boy."

"Which bothered him more? That it was a boy, or that he was Nandi?"

"Does it matter? He thought you'd been violated. So did his friends. Don't you understand what harm a scandal like this can do to a girl's reputation?" Emma's voice was bitter.

"Reputation? The only reputation I care about is how good a warrior I am. What will the Nandi think of me now, after what Daddy did?"

"Your father was protecting his good name with the only people who count up here. If you don't care about your own reputation, think of his, young lady."

"Don't call me that," said Beryl angrily.

"Beryl, look at yourself. No, I mean it: *Look* at yourself. Your body is changing. You are no longer a child to play games. You're almost a young woman."

Beryl slid down so that her chin rested on the surface of the water, but she couldn't hide what was happening to her. With her physical training, she had not missed the changes. Her chest was no longer flat. Hair was growing where it never had before. Soon her monthly bleeding would start. But that didn't mean she had to like it.

Beryl looked over at Emma, whose face was in shadow. The moment felt familiar. But that was impossible. She had never had a tub before. Then she realized that it was a time for talking, such as she had shared with Kibii many, many times. Could she possibly tell Emma her secrets? Emma! Perhaps, this one night, sitting in this remarkable tub, she could.

"I know I'm growing up," Beryl said. "But I don't want to."

"Why not?" Emma's voice was full of exasperation. "It's natural, not to say inevitable."

"Because if I become a *woman*, I can't hunt. I can't go running at night. I can't wrestle. Right now, Kibii and I are the same; we're both *totos*. Once I become a woman, then he'll become a man. And nothing will ever be the same, will it?" It was the longest speech she had ever made to Emma, and it ended with a question Beryl already knew the answer to.

Emma looked sad and triumphant at the same time. She gestured to Beryl to get out of the bath. A towel lay ready next to the tub, and she wrapped it around Beryl's body. "It's not the end of the world," she said, rubbing Beryl dry.

Beryl lifted her arms over her head to let the towel do its work and glared at Emma from under them.

"Well, for you, perhaps it is." Emma choked down a little laugh. "Let me put some iodine on that cut." She gestured for Beryl to sit on a crate. "I do understand. You don't want to give up your friendship with Kibii. But you'll have to."

Beryl opened her mouth to protest, but Emma's voice cut her off.

"Don't bother, Beryl. You could kill every lion in the highlands, but you will still be a white girl. You're the daughter of a respected landowner, his heir. You must stop humiliating him. As if your father doesn't suffer enough."

"What do you mean?"

Emma wouldn't meet Beryl's eyes, and instead busied herself smearing Beryl's thigh with iodine. Beryl held back her yelp at the sting. Emma handily wrapped the wound with gauze. As Beryl waited impatiently, Emma stowed her medical gear and then lifted the nightdress over Beryl's head.

"His position is an odd one," Emma said finally. "Since your mother left you here, people ask questions about how you're being raised."

Beryl lifted her arms and pushed them through the sleeves of the nightdress. "What blasted business is it of theirs? Daddy and I are just fine, thank you very much."

Emma took a comb and sat behind Beryl to untangle her mane of hair. "Beryl, didn't you ever wonder why I came? Your father needs to have a woman here for you."

"We don't need you," said Beryl, knowing she was being rude, just when Emma was acting rather decently.

Emma ruthlessly forced the metal comb hard through a mess of tangles.

"Ow!" said Beryl. There was no response. Finally, she glanced behind her and and was surprised to see Emma blinking back tears.

"Beryl, I know you hate me." Emma dragged the comb across Beryl's head again. "But if I hadn't come here, your father would be nagged constantly to send you away."

"No! He wouldn't do that."

Emma kept talking, unsurprised by Beryl's outburst; after all, Beryl had been shrieking "No" at her for the past year. "So I came. But since I am married to someone else, the wives of the other settlers won't come to call. That is why your father has so few visitors."

"That's the way we like it!" insisted Beryl, but she could hear the doubt in her voice.

"Your father does *not* like it," Emma retorted. "He loves parties and company. But he's an exile up here. Because of us." Her angry combing became gentler.

Beryl found herself feeling sorry for Emma. She shook herself; her shadow on the wall looked like a quivering monster.

"My father is fine. I'm fine, too." Beryl wasn't sure who she was reassuring.

"Are you fine, Beryl? Truly? Your father wants me to find out." Emma's hands had finished her deft teasing out of the tangles, and now she stroked a brush through the length of Beryl's wet hair.

"Why doesn't he ask me himself?"

"Men aren't always comfortable asking their daughters difficult questions."

Beryl didn't answer.

Emma took a deep breath. "Has Kibii ever touched you?"

"Of course he has. All the time. He taught me to wrestle."

"Has he ever . . . done more than touch you?"

"How do you mean?" Beryl wished Emma would just say what she meant.

"Well, a man . . . and a woman." Emma was overcome by embarrassment, then inspired by a new approach. "Do you know where babies come from?"

Beryl took pity on her. "Emma, I'm a farmer's daughter. I put the stallions out to stud all the time." Beryl's eyes opened wide as the point of Emma's questions finally dawned on her. "Kibii and I aren't those kind of friends."

"Are you that kind of friend with anyone?"

"No, of course not."

Emma looked relieved.

"Is there anything else that Daddy wants to know about?" Beryl's face became as guarded as any Nandi's.

"No, I don't think so."

"Good night, Emma." Beryl paused, and then remembered some remnant of her manners. "Thank you for bringing me dinner." And, as an afterthought, "And for the bathtub."

"You're welcome." Emma got up quickly, as though she couldn't get out fast enough. The door shut behind her with a bang.

Beryl sat cross-legged on her bed and began to wolf down her dinner.

The storm clouds close in, tossing my poor old <u>Messenger</u> in every direction. Each slam of air sends me off course, bit by bit. I have so little spare fuel, I dare not correct until I know where I am . . . until I sight land. I scrape the ice from the glass of my cockpit to improve my visibility. No luck.

My hand is cramped and shaking as I unscrew the top of my last thermos of coffee and pour the lukewarm liquid into a cup. A gust of wind buffets the plane and the coffee—the last of my supply—spills all over my lap.

I'm so weary, so cold. For the first time since I was a child, I am near tears.

CHAPTER EIGHTEEN

BERYL PERCHED HIGH IN THE BRANCHES OF A CEDAR TREE AND watched as the new settlers headed out on horseback. The sun beat down hard, and they wore hats to protect the bald spots on their skulls. Captain Clutterbuck was to be their guide for two weeks, perhaps more, as they inspected new settlement sites. Her father's straight back made it easy to pick him out of the crowd. But no matter how hard she willed him to, he didn't look back.

When the horses had disappeared from view, Beryl half fell, half climbed down from the tree. She must go to the village and see Kibii. It had been three days since the incident with Mehru, and she had seen no one. She had waited up each night, hoping in vain that Kibii would come.

She approached the village feeling like a stranger, unsure of her welcome. What if Mehru had been badly hurt? Was Arap Maina angry? Why had Kibii not come?

The village was deserted, except for the women minding the babies crawling in the dirt. The dogs lay sleeping in the sun, barely rousing themselves to bark at her. With relief, Beryl spied Naipende sitting under a tree, sewing beads onto a bright scarlet *shuka*.

"*Hodi*," Beryl said. It was Swahili for "I'm here, am I welcome?"

"*Kaaribu*, Beru," Naipende said in her serene way. It meant "Come, you are welcome."

Jebbta came up carrying a large pile of scarlet fabric. Beryl wondered why. The last time she had seen so many new togas, there had been a wedding in the village.

"What are you doing here, Beru?" Jebbta asked in an accusing voice.

"Since when do I need a reason, Jebbta?" Beryl shot back.

"You have caused too much trouble. You should not be here. Not after what happened to Mehru."

"Jebbta, is that any way to greet our guest?" Naipende scolded.

"Mehru wasn't hurt, was he?" Beryl said. She couldn't keep the anxiety out of her voice.

"Beru, he is fine. Just some bruises," said Naipende. Despite her reassuring words, Beryl could see that her dark eyes had worried shadows.

"Because of you, the boys have to grow up early," Jebbta blurted out.

"What are you talking about?"

"Arap Maina has decided that the boys should be circumcised this season," Naipende said, her hands busy sorting out the fabric.

"But that's wonderful—Kibii thought he would have to wait at least another year." Even as Beryl said it, she wondered if it really was good news.

"I'll have to work twice as hard," Jebbta cried. "Because there won't be any boys to help!"

"You're just upset because Mehru won't look at you once he is a *murani*," Beryl retorted.

"It's still your fault."

"Why?" asked Beryl.

After a sidelong glance at Naipende, Jebbta refused to answer.

"Naipende," Beryl said as she sank down next to the older woman. "What's going on?"

"Arap Maina was afraid that the boys would do something foolish. To avenge Mehru."

"Against Daddy?" Her father had never had trouble with his native workers, but Beryl had overheard him talking about violence in other settlements, especially the Boer colonies to the south. "Could that really happen?" she asked softly.

"The rituals will keep them busy. They have already forgotten what happened."

"Are they in the clearing?" Beryl asked.

"You cannot go there, Beru," Naipende warned gently.

"Let her go," said Jebbta spitefully. "She will soon see she is not welcome anymore."

Beryl barely heard the last words; she was running fast toward the boys. As she reached the trees that ringed the clearing, she stopped. She knew she had no place at the preparation for the male ritual. Dropping to her belly, she crawled forward in the tall grass, like a lioness stalking her prey.

Arap Maina, standing tall in his red tunic and wearing his necklaces of cable wire, was speaking to a large circle of boys. There were more than she had ever seen in the village. Arap Maina had called in all the boys from the outlying pasturage. The ritual was held only every four or five years, and many boys were waiting to become men.

Beryl edged forward so she could hear. Arap Maina's sharp eyes did not miss her arrival, and with the slightest tilt of his head, he told her to stay hidden and quiet. As soon as Beryl heard what he was saying to the *totos*, she didn't need to be told twice. He was explaining the reason for the circumcision ritual. The boys hung on every word, although they surely knew what Arap Maina was going to say.

"The pain you will feel has a deep meaning," Arap Maina said. "The cut is the break between childhood and adulthood. You will take on responsibility to protect the family and the tribe. You will be consulted on important decisions."

Kibii was in front, his back straight with pride just for being his father's son. Mehru was there, too, his right eye plastered shut with swelling and a barely healed cut across his forehead. Beryl chewed her lower lip, remembering the sound of her father's boot on Mehru's skull.

Arap Maina's kind face was at odds with his harsh message. "No matter how the cut hurts, you must not move a muscle or even blink."

Beryl touched the knife wound on her thigh and winced as she thought of the pain Kibii would feel. But she knew that it was all he dreamed of. They all did.

"The slightest movement on your part means that you are a coward and your family is disgraced." There was no comfort in Arap Maina's voice. "If you flinch, the cut will still happen, even if the elders have to hold you down."

None of the boys would look at each other. Despite their brave demeanor, Beryl could smell their fear.

"But do not despair." With a tiny shift in tone, Arap Maina again became the gentle man she knew and loved. "Every warrior in the tribe has undergone this ritual. I did not raise any of you to fail. You will support each other, as brothers."

Solemnly the boys nodded, never taking their eyes off Arap Maina.

"Next week, we will begin with the ritual of the Horn of the Ox. Now it is time to prepare. You must gather feathers for the headdress you will wear when you are a man. An elaborate headdress is a good omen for your future as a warrior. Now listen, and I will tell you how to make it."

Beryl slunk away and walked slowly back to her father's farm. No one called for her to stay. No one even noticed she was gone.

A week later, on the eve of Kibii going under the knife, Beryl slipped down to the village in the middle of the night. She went to Kibii's hut and left two enormous ostrich feathers at his door.

"Good-bye, Kibii," she whispered.

LOCATION:	Off the coast of Newfoundland, Canada

DATE:	11:50 A.M. GMT, 5 September, 1936

I check my watch. It's been nineteen hours. An hour or so ago, the sun rose in my eyes. I was never so glad to be blinded by the sun. I spot a few ships below, so I'm hopeful that I'm on course.

There! I glimpse something through the wisps of fog. There it is again: the cliffs of Newfoundland. I'm exhausted and frozen, but I feel a triumph that I haven't felt since my first lion hunt.

They said it couldn't be done. J. C. thought I was going to my death. Even my dear Tom wasn't sure I could succeed. Sitting in my cabin, I revel in the sunlight. I can see land. I'm following the wind and by my calculations, my last tank is three-quarters full.

The cliffs come closer and I'm busy calculating the distance to New York, a smile plastered across my face. I begin to sing a Nandi marching song, my voice cracking after the long solitary journey. I've made it.

When I was a child, the only stories my father told me were from mythology. I should have remembered that only the gods have the right to be confident.

The engine begins to spit and cough.

Phut, phut.

There's no more fuel. And I'm only human, like poor reckless Icarus.

CHAPTER NINETEEN

THE FROSTY MIST ROSE SLOWLY OFF THE GROUND AND FLOATED around them, seeking the sun. It would burn off soon enough, but for now, Beryl and her father were trapped in a fog where the only sound was the clopping of their horses' hooves. Beryl felt the pressure shift in the air and spotted a stork with its enormous wingspan gliding above her head. Its flight was soundless. She remembered another ride she had once taken with her father.

"If we keep up this pace, we'll be at the Elkingtons' for lunch." Her father's voice broke the silence like an egg cracking.

"It's a good thing that Emma and Little A decided not to come. They'd need the wagon, and it would take twice as long," Beryl added, watching her father's profile. Was it true that Emma wasn't welcome?

Staring straight ahead into the gloom, her father said, "Emma preferred to stay home and get some housecleaning done."

"How much more cleaning can she do?" Beryl asked.

"Never mind. Let's just ride."

Her father had returned from his trip with the settlers a week earlier, but he had still not said a word about the incident with Mehru. Waiting for him to bring up the subject, Beryl felt as though her saddle was made of tacks.

To distract herself, she stole sidelong glances to see how the Captain sat on the Baron. Beryl deliberately lengthened her reins like his, resettled herself in the saddle several times to imitate him, and practically sprained her ankles trying to keep her heels pointed down as his were. Luckily, Wee McGregor was tolerant of all her wiggling.

"Beryl, stop fidgeting. You'll drive that pony to distraction," her father snapped.

"Sorry, Daddy." But Beryl couldn't help smiling; it was such a relief to have him scold her as he usually did.

As the sun rose in the sky, Green Hills Farm was lost behind them in the summer haze, but there were still hours of riding before they would arrive at the Elkington farm. Her father reined in his gelding to ride close to her. He sighed. "You look like a wrinkled sack. Would it have been so difficult to dress up today?"

"What else should I wear? It's a long ride." Beryl's khaki trousers and white linen shirt were identical to her father's, except his had creases in all the right places. He had never abandoned the discipline he learned in the army. She tried to smooth out the wrinkles, but soon gave up.

The tranquil landscape was suddenly shaken by a lion's roar. The deep sound was several miles off, but the horses skittered nervously. Wee McGregor grabbed the bit between his teeth and tried to bolt, but Beryl was prepared for his tricks.

"That's Paddy," she said cheerfully, holding tight to the reins and pulling Wee McGregor around in a circle to keep him from running off.

"Jim Elkington is a fool," said the Captain, smacking the top of the Baron's head with a crop to bring him under control. "Whoever heard of naming a lion?"

"Paddy is Margaret's pet," Beryl said. "He's perfectly tame; it's not as though he's a wild lion."

Margaret was Jim Elkington's daughter. When Paddy's mother had been shot, Margaret had saved the cub by hand-feeding it from a bottle with milk and eggs. The lion had reached full growth by eating meat that Elkington's workers caught for him.

Beryl was fascinated by Paddy. She had often watched the lion wandering Mr. Jim's farm like an emperor surveying his domain. He always walked alone. He had never seen the inside of a cage, but he reeked of humans and he would never be accepted by wild lions.

Her father snorted. "A tame lion is an unnatural lion—and untrustworthy. Beryl, don't you ever forget that."

"I'm not afraid," she assured him.

The Captain pulled his horse in front of Beryl's and grabbed Wee McGregor's bridle. "Young lady, I know you're brave enough. Going on that fool lion hunt proved that. But even warriors show some caution. Watch yourself around that lion."

She nodded without saying anything. He stared at her with his stern gray eyes, unsatisfied with what he saw. "Beryl Clutterbuck, I'm not certain the Le May woman was totally at fault. I think you asked for the trouble she gave you."

"But Daddy! She was awful!"

"And ugly to boot. But don't tell Emma I said so." They grinned at each other. "And I know you were just defending yourself from that boy, what was his name?"

"Mehru."

"But you seem to find danger wherever you go. Today, let's not go looking for it, all right?"

Beryl bobbed her head more enthusiastically this time. The Captain kicked his horse into a canter. The sun beating down on their backs, they galloped toward the roaring of the tame lion.

They arrived at the farm in the middle of the afternoon. The Captain's new Indian servant, Bishon Singh, had arrived the night before and was waiting for them. He held their bridles as they dismounted. Mr. Jim came down from the house to greet them. He was a bald man and very round—but his roundness was muscle, not fat. His belt was a strip of rhino leather he had cured himself. His *kiboko*, cut from the same rhino hide, was coiled and hung on a loop at his hip. Mr. Jim was no gentleman farmer, ordering the natives to do the dangerous work—he did it himself.

His daughter, Margaret, trailed behind her bulky father, almost hopping with excitement at seeing Beryl. She waited for the adults to walk away and then rushed up to Beryl, who was sitting on the edge of a trough pulling off her sweaty riding boots, followed by her dirty socks.

"Hello, Beryl." Margaret looked down at Beryl's bare feet with a frown crinkling her pale forehead.

"Margaret," Beryl replied.

"I thought you'd never get here," she said. "You haven't been here in almost a year."

Beryl said indifferently, "You could always visit us."

Margaret shook her head, "Oh, no. My mother would never permit it."

"Why not?" Beryl asked.

"She says your household is irregular." Margaret sounded puzzled, as though she were parroting an adult conversation she hadn't understood.

"What does that mean?" Beryl asked warily.

"I don't know." Margaret twirled around, making her skirt flare. "Do you like my new dress?" She wore a frilly white tea dress and a straw hat with another white ribbon around the crown, carefully protecting her skin from the sun.

Mrs. Elkington often said that Margaret and Beryl could be twins, since they were both tall with long blond hair. But Beryl's hair was a wild mess, while Margaret's was neatly plaited with white ribbons.

"It's only last year's fashion," Margaret said proudly.

"It's very nice," Beryl lied.

"I wish we could get the latest styles more quickly—it takes forever!"

"Why do you care about what's fashionable two continents away?"

"You don't know anything, Beryl."

"I know that fashion is stupid." Beryl started toward the house.

"Didn't you bring shoes?" Margaret asked.

"Why?" Beryl asked. She looked down at her stained and callused feet. "I always walk barefoot. You couldn't stalk a warthog with your squeaky boots."

"Why would I. . . . Never mind, Beryl. I don't know why I bothered. Come have tea; I baked shortbread and gingersnaps."

After the long ride, the thought of cakes and biscuits set Beryl's mouth to watering, so she willingly followed Margaret behind their house. Beryl always laughed when she saw their garden. Mrs. Elkington had tried to create an English garden with white-painted lawn furniture and a bone china tea set. The illusion worked, until you looked beyond the patch of cultivated grass that needed hand watering from the well twice a day in the dry season. Africa didn't go away just because you pretended it wasn't there.

The men gathered in a circle around her father. The Captain chuckled at one of Mr. Jim's jokes. Next to Mr. Jim's cannonball shape, the Captain looked like a white Nandi warrior, straight as a spear. Beryl sidled over to listen. They were talking solemnly of politics in faraway England, the price of grain, and the prospects for the Nairobi St. Leger horse race. The few women present were fussing about a table covered in blindingly white linen. Beryl examined the treats they were arranging on platters, pretending not to notice how the adult women were looking her over and exchanging knowing glances.

Margaret began pouring tea from a silver pot and offering one lump or two of sugar to the guests. Beryl hovered, waiting for her sweets so she could escape. Even though the party was outside, she found it hard to breathe. The conversation, the manners, even the bone china seemed to suck away her air. She practically grabbed a plate out of Margaret's hands and backed quickly away, mumbling her thanks. Reaching the veranda, she edged around the corner. Out of sight of the others, she shoved the pastries in her mouth. Licking her lips, she took a good look around.

The Elkington farm was at the edge of the Kikuyu Reserve. The country looked different here. There was no forest, just plains. Beryl began to explore, her body carving its way through the hazy air like the sharp edge of her knife. As she ran through a stand of trees, her feet crunched the dead cicadas on the ground. What she found on the other side stopped her in her tracks.

Paddy the lion was sprawled there without a care in the world.

As lions go, he was quite small. But the last time she had faced a lion, Arap Maina and Tepli had been there. And they had nearly died. Paddy was only a few yards away; nothing compared to the distance he could leap if he chose. She stared at his black mane and his rusty red fur. She remembered stroking that fur when he was a cub.

"Remember me, Paddy?" she whispered. "We used to be friends."

He lifted his large head and stared at Beryl through his heavy-lidded yellow eyes. The only sound she heard was the thumping of his tail on the dry ground. Beryl fought to control the panic welling up in her stomach.

Very casually, almost as if she were scratching an itch, she reached down to her calf and pulled her knife out of its sheath. Her father's description of a tame lion, "untrustworthy," hung in the haze. Paddy shimmered in the waves of heat. She took careful, measured steps and started to walk past him.

To show Paddy that she was not afraid, she began to sing a marching song that Arap Maina had taught her. She sang in Swahili, so Paddy would be sure to understand.

Kali coma simba sisi
A sikari yoti ni udari!
Fierce like the lion are we,
Warriors, all are brave.

Perhaps she imagined it, but the tuft at the end of Paddy's weighty tail seemed to beat time with her song. Her voice cracking with the strain of sounding braver than she felt, she went past him, up the hill, out of his line of sight.

Once on the other side of the hill, she bent over, breathing deeply to settle her stomach. She had been lucky, she thought, as she replaced her knife in its sheath. Looking out over the hot and dry horizon, she noticed that there was no wind to stir the grass. For all its teeming life, Africa was often silent, as it was that day.

Beryl began to practice running on the balls of her feet, quietly, as Tepli had taught her. Suddenly, she heard a low growl behind her. She whirled around. Paddy raced up the hill toward her, making hardly any noise. He gathered his haunches and leapt. Beryl went down under his massive paws as easily as if she were a gazelle. His large fangs sank into the flesh of her right leg.

Paddy lifted his head and slammed Beryl onto the earth. Beryl opened her mouth to scream, but her cry was ground into the dirt. Paddy's musky smell blocked everything else. His weight settled on her back; she could feel the claws of his hind paws behind her neck. An immense roar became her whole world.

From very far away, she could hear the voices of men. Bishon Singh was shrieking for help. Mr. Jim's shouts were punctuated with the whistling crack of his *kiboko*.

Paddy's teeth slipped out of Beryl's calf as he turned his heavy head to look at the intruder. The pain in her leg stabbed like a knife. Her body shook with the rumbling of his angry growl. Suddenly, his claws were pushing off Beryl's body as he abandoned his prey and faced the new enemy.

Beryl dared to open her eyes in time to see Mr. Jim rush headlong at Paddy. But Paddy didn't back down. Beryl struggled to stand on her throbbing leg. Her head swam. Suddenly Bishon Singh's hands were on her, scooping her off the ground. He threw her over his shoulder and started running.

As she bounced, she could see Mr. Jim and Paddy circling each other like duelists. Paddy roared his terrible roar. To Beryl's surprise, Mr. Jim lost his nerve. He dropped the whip and clambered up the nearest tree.

Then Bishon Singh carried her away and all was nothingness.

"So what happened next?" Beryl asked Bishon Singh. She lay in a soft bed in a room with white organza curtains. Her wounds were bandaged, and her head was befuddled with liberal doses of whiskey administered to numb the pain.

Bishon Singh dipped his head so low that Beryl feared his massive turban might tumble off. "Miss Beryl, I was happy with the duty of advising your father that you had been moderately eaten by the large lion. Your father returned very fast. But the large lion has not returned at all."

The next day, Margaret came in to change Beryl's bandages.

"Hello, Margaret," Beryl said cheerfully. "How's Paddy?"

"They didn't find him until yesterday," she said. "But only after he killed a cow, a horse, and a bullock."

Beryl burst out laughing. "I've always thought that meat you hunted yourself tasted better."

"You don't understand, Beryl." Margaret looked up from Beryl's leg, where she was unwinding the bandages. Her eyes were red from weeping. "Papa says he has to stay in a cage now. Forever!"

Beryl was silent, remembering how she felt when Miss Le May locked her in her hut.

Margaret went on, "And it's all your fault!"

"My fault?" Beryl asked, suddenly angry. "I was mauled!"

"You know better than to tempt Paddy like that—running past him like a rabbit in those bare feet. He was a good lion until you came."

Beryl started to protest, but stopped. If she hadn't been so reckless, would Paddy have attacked?

Margaret finished unwrapping Beryl's leg. She looked down at the assortment of punctures. "It's only a scratch," she sniffed. "It's not like you won't be able to walk."

Beryl sat up and looked down at the ugly red wounds. "Are you insane? Paddy tried to eat me!"

"And thanks to you, he'll die in a cage!" And to Beryl's surprise, Margaret burst into tears and ran howling out of the room.

A few days later, Beryl was well enough to ride home. She followed Paddy's plaintive roar to find the noble beast imprisoned in a too-small cage behind the stables. When Paddy saw Beryl, he stopped roaring and stared at her with dulled eyes.

Beryl's own eyes filled with tears as she saw that he no longer looked at her as prey. "I'm sorry, Paddy," she whispered. "I know you were just taking your chance to be a wild lion."

"His only chance, as it turns out." The Captain came up behind her. "Jim Elkington promises to keep him locked up for good."

Beryl felt a pang in her chest. "Oh, Daddy, he couldn't help attacking me—it's in his nature."

"Just as it is in yours to risk your neck. Well, no more. I'm clipping your wings."

As though the cage door had clanged behind her, Beryl whirled around to face her father. "What do you mean?"

"You're going away to school. I can't trust you to keep out of trouble if you stay up here."

"Did Emma . . ." Beryl began angrily.

"Beryl—you brought this on yourself." The steel in her father's voice silenced her. "You could easily have been killed last month, last week, two days ago. No argument. You go to Nairobi as soon as Emma can get you packed."

They mounted their horses. Beryl thought furiously as they rode. They had covered several miles before she spoke again. "Daddy, I don't need to go to school."

"Beryl, the subject is closed."

"I want to stay up here."

"No."

The horses clip-clopped for half a mile or so before she tried again.

"Daddy, I'm not my mother to be frightened away, or Emma to cower in the house. I want to be your partner on the farm."

"You're too young," he said automatically. Then he did a double take. "How old are you now?"

"I don't keep track," Beryl answered. This wasn't the time to remind him that she was only twelve. Another birthday had come and gone without anyone at Green Hills Farm, including Beryl, taking notice.

She went on, "But I'll tell you one thing: If I were a Nandi girl, I could be married now."

"If you were a Nandi girl, I wouldn't have to worry about you getting into trouble." The Captain went on, and his voice was suddenly bleak, "You could have been killed by that lion."

"What if I gave up hunting?" Beryl offered.

"Beryl, it's not enough. I have a reputation to worry about. It makes me look eccentric if you don't get an education." His tone was final.

Beryl wondered if she could salvage anything. "How much education do I need?" she asked. "I don't want to go to university— I want to stay in Africa and help you run the farm."

"You'll need more mathematics if you are to help me with the books." It was a tiny crack in his resolve—Beryl wasted no time driving in a wedge.

"So, three months of arithmetic and I'd be ready."

"Two years," he countered.

"Six months should be plenty. I'll study hard."

"One year, and that's as low as I go—Emma will insist on that much."

"Agreed. A year."

"But if you don't last a year, I'll . . ." The Captain trailed off, trying to think of the most awful punishment he could devise. Finally his eyes lit up: "I'll send you to your mother in England!"

Swallowing hard, Beryl nodded.

During the rest of the ride, Beryl had time to consider the bargain she had made. Her taunting of Paddy had cost her a year of schooling—but the lion would live out the rest of his life in a cage. They had both paid for her folly with their freedom.

My engine is shuddering. Then it coughs, spitting black exhaust toward the sea. I watch my hands working furiously, as if they aren't attached to my body. When the engine stops, the sudden silence stuns me. I can't feel fear. I can't feel anything.

It has to be an airlock—a bubble of air in the tubes, blocking the fuel flow. I open and close all the petcocks, cutting my fingers on the sharp metal edges. The engine catches again and roars back to life. I climb. North

America is close enough to see, but perhaps too far to fly to. The engine cuts out and I glide down toward the cliffs of Newfoundland.

On. Off. Stop. Go. Each minute brings me closer to the airport at Cape Breton. Seesawing between life and death, I'm hypnotized by the altimeter. I'm over land, gliding over green pasture. The airport must be close.

One more time, little Messenger. Just start for me one more time.

CHAPTER TWENTY

"YOUR FATHER IS A COWARD," EMMA SAID TO BERYL AS THEY boarded the train at Nakuru.

Her stomach twisted in a bitter knot, Beryl didn't try to defend the Captain. At the last minute, he had made a feeble excuse not to accompany her to school and had sent Emma in his place. While the other passengers chatted, played cards, and sipped from flasks, Beryl and Emma had spoken perhaps ten words during the long, bone-jarring trip. On her previous trips to Nairobi, Beryl had never thought of the train ride as uncomfortable. But then she had always been with her father, and she had had a return ticket.

When the train pulled into Nairobi, Emma fixed her dark hair, now reddish with dust. After she washed her face, she looked happier than Beryl had ever seen her. "I love the city," she said.

They walked out of the station onto the street, followed by a porter hauling Beryl's trunk and Emma's suitcase. The sun had already set, but the streets were filled with carriages and people. There were even a few of those noisy new automobiles. Beryl put her hands over her ears.

"Stop that, Beryl. You look ridiculous," Emma snapped as the porter flagged a rickshaw for them. "The Nairobi School for European Children," she ordered the driver.

"Yes, memsahib." The rickshaw driver bundled them into the narrow seat. He sighed when he looked at Beryl's heavy trunk. The porter helped him lift it and secure it to the back of the cart. Then the driver grabbed hold of the handles and, with a heave, began pulling Beryl toward her new life.

The school was at the top of a hill overlooking what had become downtown. If Beryl had not been so miserable, she might have exclaimed at how much bigger the city had grown. A few years ago, it had been burned to the ground to fight a plague. But the city had already rebuilt itself and gotten even bigger.

It was fully dark by the time Emma and Beryl arrived at the school. Even high up on a hill, and after the sun had set, the muggy heat weighed on Beryl's skin. Stiff from the long journey, she unfolded her long legs and got out of the rickshaw. She let the driver help Emma out.

"Wait here," Emma said the driver. "I won't be long."

Beryl stared at her new home. The school looked like the letter E with the middle stroke removed. It sat on stilts, and Beryl could not see what was underneath. A door opened wide at the top of the wooden stairs in the center of the building, and a slim figure appeared. She was holding a lantern, which spilled light down to Beryl and Emma.

A high-pitched nasal voice called out, "Hello, Clutterbucks! I was afraid that awful train had finally broken down in the wilderness. Come up, come up! You must be exhausted. Watch your step—these stairs are steep, but we find that the building stays cooler off the ground."

It was the proprietress herself, Miss Seccombe. Beryl and Emma blinked at her, their eyes adjusting to the light of the paraffin lantern. Miss Seccombe was a slight woman with a pasty face. Her brown hair was gathered underneath a cotton kerchief. She ushered them into a tiny parlor that smelled of furniture polish.

"Sit down," she said, gesturing to an overstuffed sofa.

When she sat down, Beryl discovered that the sofa wasn't as comfortable as it looked. Emma settled in next to her, placing her gray-gloved hand over Beryl's scratched brown hand. Beryl pulled her hand away. Emma sighed.

Miss Seccombe smiled, revealing a healthy amount of teeth; Beryl was reminded of a hyena's grin. She spoke only to Emma.

"My school accepts only children from the best British families. There are seven other girls her age. We teach boys as well, but they are confined to their half of the school with their own dormitory, teacher, and classroom." She pushed toward them a tray that held glasses of lemonade. "I'm sure Beryl will be happy here, Mrs. Clutterbuck."

Before Emma could reply, Beryl croaked, "She's not my father's wife—don't call her Clutterbuck." Then she began coughing from the dust and her long silence. She took the glass in front of her and gulped it down.

There was an embarrassed silence before Emma found her voice. "I'm not Beryl's mother, Miss Seccombe. I help her father with the housekeeping."

Miss Seccombe looked at Emma's white cotton traveling dress and fashionable hat. "Oh, I see." She looked down her pointy nose. "Well then, Miss . . ."

"*Mrs.* Orchardson," corrected Emma.

Beryl glared at her; this was the first she had heard of Emma's husband since Emma had arrived over a year ago.

Miss Seccombe coughed. "Mrs. Orchardson, would you like to see the school? It's late for a tour, but I can . . ."

Emma said hurriedly, "No, no. I've delivered Beryl. I must be going to the hotel." She hesitated and then put her arms around Beryl in an awkward embrace. Beryl kept her arms straight at her sides. Emma whispered, "Behave yourself, Beryl. Your father sends you his love." She said a quick farewell to Miss Seccombe and was gone.

Beryl couldn't help feeling abandoned as the echo of Emma's steps faded in the stairway. Before the door had slammed closed, the headmistress's smile had disappeared. Holding her lantern high, she led Beryl into a narrow hallway. Miss Seccombe pointed to the left. "That is the boys' wing. The girls are down here." The lantern threw strange shadows on the whitewashed walls.

"Miss Clutterbuck, there are a few rules I expect you to abide by during your time here." Miss Seccombe pointed to a hand-lettered sign on the wall.

* You shall not blaspheme.
* You shall not tell falsehoods.
* You shall not disrespect the faculty.
* You shall not leave the premises without permission.
* You shall not resort to violence.

"Break these rules and you face severe disciplinary action, perhaps even expulsion."

Beryl found comfort in the rules—who knew it was so easy to be expelled? She thought longingly of Arap Maina, of following him into the forest, learning to imitate animal noises, practicing her wrestling moves. Arap Maina taught by example, not with lists of stupid rules.

"Your father wrote that you have lacked a certain discipline in the past, Beryl. That won't be tolerated here."

"Yes, ma'am," said Beryl in a low voice, flexing her hands that had once taken so much "discipline" from Miss Le May.

"Don't mutter, dear," admonished Miss Seccombe. "And don't clench your fists."

"Yes, ma'am," Beryl muttered.

"This is the girls' dormitory." Miss Seccombe opened the door to a long room with beds lined up in a row against the wall. Half a dozen or so girls, clad in long white nightgowns, were preparing for bed by the light of two candles. When the door opened, they fell silent.

"This is your bed," Miss Seccombe said, pointing to a bed at the end. "You can put your clothes in this chest." She opened it and clucked her tongue. "Whose things are these? Each girl gets one chest. Who is using Beryl's?"

A girl with long black hair and a turned-up nose flipped back her bedcovers and hopped out of bed. "They're my things, Miss Seccombe."

"Mary, how many times have I told you . . . ?"

"But there isn't room for all my clothes," the girl protested.

"Remove them," said Miss Seccombe.

Beryl said, "I haven't brought many clothes; she can have it if she wants it." Actually, Beryl had no idea what she had brought. Emma had supervised the packing.

"Beryl that is very generous of you—but Mary knows the rules."

Mary gave Beryl a baleful look, opened the chest, pulled out her dresses, and took them away to her own dresser. Mary's hair was something to see. It was divided into a dozen plaits, each twisted around a damp rag, like a crop of black snakes had sprouted on her head. Beryl remembered a story her father had told her of Medusa. She wondered whether Mary was as dangerous.

"Beryl, the other girls can show you the outhouse and explain the morning schedule." Handing Beryl a candle, Miss Seccombe left the room, leaving her surrounded by more girls than she had ever been with in her life. Their eyes gleamed in the dim room like predators in the forest. She was outnumbered and out of her element. Deep in the privacy of her own mind she chanted, "I'm a *murani*, I'm a *murani*."

The girl with too many clothes stepped forward. "I'm Mary Russell—who are you?"

"Beryl Clutterbuck."

"Clutterbuck? I've never heard of you."

A short girl with brown curly hair spoke up. "Clutterbuck? Captain Clutt? The racehorse trainer?"

"He's my father," Beryl said, cheered that someone knew about things that mattered.

"My father wants to buy one of his horses. He says the Captain raises the best."

"Does he want a mare or a gelding?" Beryl asked eagerly. "I know every horse, and I . . ."

Mary interrupted. "Enough about horses. Raising horses is hardly a gentleman's profession."

Beryl bristled. "So what does your father do that is so gentlemanly?"

Mary tossed back her ragged snakes. "Nothing, of course. He lives off his income!"

The other girls tittered. Furious that she had given Mary a chance to make fun of her, Beryl asked, "What's he doing in Africa, then? Waiting on his remittance check?"

The other girls gasped. Remittance men were the black sheep of good families whose relatives happily paid them an allowance to stay far away from England. After the initial shock, the girls began to laugh. The girl who had asked about horses laughed harder than the others.

"Mary, watch your step with this one." She formally held out her hand to Beryl and introduced herself. "I'm Doris Waterman."

Mary's angry cheeks had two high spots of color, visible even in the candlelight. "I really had better watch my step—Beryl's brought in manure on her shoes. Can't you smell it?"

Beryl clenched her fists so that her nails dug into her palms. Trying to seem unconcerned, she lifted a foot to her nose and sniffed. Effortlessly, she switched feet and sniffed again. She shrugged. The other girls stared, stunned that she could pull her foot so high so effortlessly.

Mary tried again. "Are you sure you are in the right room? With those trousers and man's shirt—maybe you should be in the boys' dormitory?"

Beryl looked down at her khaki breeches and white linen shirt. She hadn't bothered to change after her last ride on Camiscan.

Mary clearly meant to be rude, but Beryl couldn't see where the insult was. She glanced around at the strange girls. "I'd rather wear comfortable clothes than a stupid dress," she muttered.

"Oh, you'll wear a dress. Miss Seccombe will insist. You'll have to make lots of changes to fit in with us. But you will change," Mary promised. "I guarantee it."

The thought of stockings, stays, tight shoes, dresses, and hats brought home Beryl's new situation. Tears welled up in her eyes. Dashing them away with the back of her hand, she opened her mouth to say something cutting to Mary, but no sound came out.

Mary took advantage of her silence and announced, "Lights out!" She bent over and blew out Beryl's candle. On her signal, someone extinguished the second candle. Beryl was left alone in the dark.

Without bothering to undress, she reached into her satchel and unerringly picked out the one bundle she cared about. Her lion's paw was wrapped in an old linen handkerchief. It had been smuggled in after Emma had approved the packing.

Beryl threw her body onto the unfamiliar bed. Having never used a pillow before, she tossed it to the floor. The straw ticking of the mattress felt itchy through the cotton sheet. She lay in the dark, stroking the furry paw over and over. She longed for her usual lullaby of hyraxes, hyenas, and cicadas, but instead the snores of seven other girls, more threatening than any roar, kept her awake.

LOCATION: A peat bog, Baleine Cove, Nova Scotia, Canada

DATE: 10:10 A.M. EST, 5 September, 1936

The Messenger won't start. It's dead as death. I hang above the earth on hope and a motionless propeller. The earth rushes to me. Can I lose enough speed to land safely?

The wheels touch the green ground, and for a moment, I think I've made it. But even the ground has betrayed me. It isn't solid. My wheels skim along the surface for perhaps forty feet, but they find no purchase. They sink and the nose crashes forward into the mud. I strike my head on the glass of the cockpit. I hear it shatter and feel a sharp pain on my forehead. Then nothing.

After a time—I don't know how long—my eyes open. I blink against the brightness. There's wetness on my forehead. I touch it. I'm relieved beyond measure to see it is blood. Dead pilots don't bleed.

I unstrap my harness and stumble out. Standing knee-deep in the bog, I can only stare at my watch. Twenty-one hours and 25 minutes.

CHAPTER TWENTY-ONE

"STUDENTS, TAKE YOUR SEATS."

Miss Seccombe clapped her hands briskly to get the girls' attention. In daylight, her wispy grayish-brown hair was pulled back so tight that it stretched her small face out to the hairline like an elastic band.

With a sigh, Beryl turned her gaze from the window and back into the large classroom. The wide planks of the floor were fastened together by iron brackets recessed into the wood, making the floor resemble a railroad track. Cumbersome wooden desks were laid out in precise rows, and white porcelain inkwells perched on the tops of the desks like warts. Wincing from her new black patent-leather boots, Beryl moved to her desk. She rubbed her nose, and the smell of flowery soap Miss Seccombe had insisted she use made her sneeze.

"Get out your books."

Beryl lifted the heavy lid and pulled out her pen and books. She let the lid slam down with a bang.

"Miss Clutterbuck, is that noise necessary?" asked Miss Seccombe.

"No, ma'am," muttered Beryl.

The other girls tittered. They did that a lot. Beryl thought they sounded like colubus monkeys. If she closed her eyes, she almost felt she was at home.

Miss Seccombe cleared her throat. "Before we begin, I have a special announcement."

The class stirred expectantly.

"As you know, the class will be performing *Alice in Wonderland* for the holiday play. I think it will be a lovely welcome to our new student, Beryl, if she plays Alice."

There were muffled gasps from the other girls. Mary stood up in indignation, shoving her desk across the floor with a loud squeak. "Miss Seccombe, *I* was to play Alice."

"I know, dear." Miss Seccombe smiled her hyena smile. "But it's someone else's turn to play the lead."

Doris piped up, "Beryl looks the part more than you do, Mary." There was a chorus of agreement from the others. Beryl, who had never heard of *Alice in Wonderland*, was too bewildered to say anything. Mary's face was flushed, and there were tears in her eyes.

"But Miss Seccombe . . ." Mary wailed.

"Take out your books," said Miss Seccombe, ending the debate.

First the class read a passage in their primers about two sisters named Polly and Molly, and a tea party at a parsonage. Then Miss Seccombe lifted her bell, her signal that the class was moving on to something else. Beryl was used to telling time by the position of the sun. Even her father's preoccupation with his pocket watch was less irritating than the tinkling of Miss Seccombe's bell.

"Girls, for composition, I want you to write an essay about

a moment that changed your life. I'll give you an hour for your first draft."

Even though it was her first essay, Beryl didn't pause to consider her subject. She knew exactly what to say. With a decisive nod, she dipped the nib of her pen into the inkwell and began to write busily, filling up page after page.

Miss Seccombe rang her little bell. "Excellent concentration, girls. Who would like to read her essay first?"

Beryl was not surprised to see Mary's hand shoot up. With a resigned nod, Miss Seccombe told her to begin.

Mary stood up, her starched cotton dress falling perfectly straight without a single wrinkle. Her hair was neatly gathered with a bow, so her black curls cascaded down her back. In a high artificial voice, she recited:

> *"The moment that changed my life was the day my grandmother*
> *sent me a dress from Paris. My father told me I looked like*
> *Princess Mary and he took me to tea at the New Stanley Hotel.*
> *The manager came out to greet us and lead us to the best table.*
> *We had tea from India and biscuits from London."*

Beryl stopped listening and let her mind drift to Green Hills Farm. As though she were picking at a scab, she mentally listed all the favorite activities she had already missed that day: waking to the sun coming up over the mountains; the clean, cold alpine air; early morning workout with the horses . . .

Finally, Mary finished and Doris stood up. She talked about taking a ship from Dover to Mombasa. Beryl, who had been only two years old when she had made the same journey with her parents, rather enjoyed Doris's essay.

Finally, Miss Seccombe called on Beryl. In a clear clipped voice, Beryl began:

"Several months ago I hunted a lion with the Nandi warriors on my father's farm. I was the first girl they ever let go with them. My best friend, Kibii, the leader's son, was not allowed to come . . ."

From Beryl's first words, the class was spellbound. Mary tried to snicker, but the others hushed her.

"I walked home with the lion's paw stuck on my spear. I was a murani*!"*

Beryl looked around the room with a huge grin. If she couldn't be at home, writing about it had been an unexpected comfort. The other girls' faces wore stunned and admiring looks. Doris's eyes were shining and her mouth was voicelessly shaping the words, "I was a *murani*."

Then Beryl saw Miss Seccombe's face, which was frozen in what could only be described as horror. "Miss Clutterbuck, the assignment was to write a *true* story."

Beryl stared down at Miss Seccombe. She imagined her blue eyes were gimlets drilling into the teacher's puny head. "Every word was God's own truth," she said.

"I don't permit blasphemy, either," said Miss Seccombe in a cold voice. "How dare you use the Lord's name to justify your lies?"

The other girls' mouths hung open.

Beryl said, "I can prove it."

The girls began whispering and giggling. Beryl ignored them and limped out of the room, wincing when her shoes pinched her feet.

"Where are you going?" Miss Seccombe squeaked.

"To get proof," Beryl said without pausing.

When she returned, Miss Seccombe was still ringing her bell to calm the classroom. Silence fell completely as Beryl carefully placed a linen bundle on Miss Seccombe's desk.

She gestured to Miss Seccombe to unfold the cloth. Miss Seccombe shook her head warily and put her hands in the wide pockets of her skirt. Smirking, Beryl opened the bundle herself. Triumphantly, she held up the dried-out lion's paw. She stood proud, daring anyone to doubt her word again.

Miss Seccombe's eyes rolled to the backs of their sockets and she fanned herself with her handkerchief. Mary shrieked and backed away. Doris led the rest of the girls in a rush to get a closer look.

Finally Miss Seccombe found her voice. "Miss Clutterbuck, we're going to need new rules for you. It never occurred to me to prohibit wild animal body parts in school. That—that—*thing* is confiscated!"

"No!" Beryl shrieked. "It's mine. I earned it! You can't take it!" She dropped into a warrior's crouch, one arm raised as if she were carrying her buffalo-skin shield, ready to defend her prize. Her hand slapped at her skirt, but Emma had made sure Beryl's knife had not made the journey to Nairobi. She had managed to bring only a small sharp pocketknife, and that was hidden in her chest in the dormitory.

"Give it over, young lady," insisted Miss Seccombe. Looking more closely at Beryl's defiant face, she added grudgingly, "You can have it back when you return home."

Beryl was too angry to believe her, and edged forward to snatch it.

Doris grabbed her arm and dragged her back. "Beryl, leave it," she whispered. "You'll get it back."

Beryl took her eyes off the lion's paw and looked down at Doris's hand on her arm.

"You'll get it back," Doris repeated. "But if you fight her, you'll never see it again."

Slowly Beryl's body lost its tension and she stepped away from the desk. Her shoulders slumped and even her hair felt as though it were weighing her down, trapping her here.

Miss Seccombe gingerly grabbed a linen corner between two fingers and folded it over the paw. Her lips pursed tightly, she held the bundle far from her body and scurried out of the room. When she returned, she gave Beryl a look filled with dislike. "Miss Clutterbuck, you will stand in the corner. You may not participate in our spelling lesson."

Beryl kept her face blank as she walked over to the corner and faced the window.

"Not to the window, Beryl. To the wall. Letting you daydream would be no punishment at all."

Beryl stood facing the wall, wriggling uncomfortably in her scratchy clothing. Under her wide skirt, one leg was bent as she stood in the Nandi way. For the next hour, Beryl imagined she was a huge bird, soaring back to the highlands, the train chugging slowly beneath her. She heard the far-off whistle of the train and wasn't sure if it was real or her imagination.

Finally Beryl was released to recess by the tinkle of the little bell. She was the first out the door. Inhaling deeply, she looked around the dusty yard, searching for possible escape routes. Doris's voice at her shoulder startled her.

"We all play skip rope at recess. Do you want to join us, Beryl?"

Beryl looked at the group of girls. The hostility from the night before was gone. Most of them were watching Beryl curiously. Except Mary. She stood to one side, pretending not to notice that Beryl was being included by the others.

"Skip rope?" asked Beryl. "How do you do it?"

"Haven't you ever skipped rope before?" Doris asked in a surprised voice.

"I'm sure I can do it—just tell me how you win."

The girls giggled again like monkeys. Beryl ground her teeth and waited for Doris to explain the rules.

"You don't win. Two of us turn the rope, and you hop over the rope when it hits the ground. We all sing the rhyme."

"Why?" Beryl asked. "To strengthen muscles?"

"In the civilized world, we do things for fun," Mary said. "Feel free *not* to join us."

Doris stepped forward. "Mary, be quiet. Give Beryl a chance."

There was a murmur of agreement from the other girls.

Doris was being decent, and Mary didn't want Beryl to play. That was reason enough for Beryl to join in. "I'll try."

Doris nodded. "All right." She pointed to Mary with a mischievous gleam in her eyes. "Mary, you take this end, and I'll take the other. Beryl, don't worry if you trip at first—it happens to everyone."

The girls began turning the rope. Beryl studied the way it came down and flopped on the ground and then rose again in an arc. Once she understood how it worked, she jumped in. The girls started chanting in time to the snap of the rope on the dusty ground.

Grace, Grace, dressed in lace,
Went upstairs to powder her face.
How many boxes did it take?
One, two, three, four . . .

Beryl's feet were fast, even in the tight shoes. She didn't miss a hop. In the back of her mind, she blocked out the high-pitched chanting of the girls. In its place, she hummed the Kikuyu jumping song to keep the rhythm.

"Ninety-eight, ninety-nine, one hundred." As the weary voices of the girls reached the century mark, Beryl leapt high in the air and landed perfectly with both feet planted on the rope. The girls gaped for a moment, and then deliberately turned their backs and walked away. Doris stayed there, chewing on her lip.

"What's wrong?" Beryl asked.

Mary was still holding the rope. She gave it a hard tug. Beryl, staring after the others, was taken unawares. She fell to the ground, her feet splayed and her skirt askew. She glared angrily at Mary, who was doubled over with laughter.

"You look ridiculous," Mary taunted. "And I don't believe that you hunted a lion!"

Beryl lunged over to grab her ankle and twist—a Nandi wrestling move guaranteed to bring down an opponent standing above you. But she got tangled in her skirt and fell down again into the dirt. To her fury, Mary laughed harder.

"Oh, Beryl! If Miss Seccombe could see you now, she would never cast you in my part." She sashayed over to the others, leaving Beryl lying in the dirt, fuming.

Still holding the rope, Doris looked thoughtful. Beryl looked up at her and asked, "Why did they go? Didn't I do it right?"

Doris dropped the rope. "Beryl—in skip rope, we take turns. If you never miss, no one else gets a turn." She hesitated, as though there was more she wanted to say, then shrugged and left Beryl in the dirt, alone.

Beryl passed the rest of the day without speaking a word. When she returned to the dormitory that evening, the room fell silent the instant she walked in. The hairs on the back of her neck stood on end as her eyes darted around the room. The girls avoided looking at her, particularly Mary.

Ignoring them as best she could, Beryl strode over to her bed to strip off the itchy coverlet.

As she lifted the pillow, she sucked in a hiss of surprise. A long, thick snake lay coiled in a tight circle. Its yellow skin was dotted with brown spots. It snapped at her, its forked tongue tasting her scent. She looked closer at the snake—it was harmless, a sand boa. Behind her, Beryl could hear the smothered giggles of the other girls. Her lips turned up in a wicked smile; she had an idea.

"Good heavens!" she exclaimed in a near-falsetto, "I wonder how that got here. It's a *joka*! It's not poisonous, except for its skin. Anyone who touches it will break out in boils soon after. And if they don't wash their hands constantly for two days . . ." She paused.

A strangled voice, just barely identifiable as Mary's, asked, "What? What will happen?"

With a solemn air, Beryl said, "She might lose the hand." She picked up a ruler and, with exaggerated care, slid it under the snake to lift it by its middle and headed out of the dormitory. She closed the door behind her and listened to Mary's panicked voice and the splash of water in the washbasin.

Giggling to herself, Beryl draped the snake around her shoulders and sneaked down the hallway, grateful that she had learned to walk so silently. She tiptoed past Miss Seccombe's study and ran down the back stairs to ease herself and the snake into the pale darkness of the Nairobi night.

Beryl walked down the road, away from the city lights and the school. She stopped next to a stand of trees with a thicket of flowering bushes underneath. Sinking down to the ground, she crossed her legs underneath her ridiculous billowing nightgown.

"I wish I could have seen Mary's face," she confided to the snake. "But I didn't trust myself not to give the show away." She ran a forefinger across the back of its head. "I wish you could talk. I could use a friend." The snake gave a convulsive shudder, took a last snap at her finger, and slithered off her shoulders to disappear into the thicket.

Beryl leaned back against the tree and looked up at the night sky. She and Kibii used to look at the stars together. She knew that home was only ninety miles away, but her old friends, the constellations, shivered in the pale sky like strangers, obscured by the lights and smoke of Nairobi. What was Kibii doing now? she wondered. Was he a warrior yet?

"Beryl! Beryl!" A voice whispered her name. Startled, Beryl looked up at the sky. Then she realized the voice was coming from a small figure walking toward her. Her hand went to the dagger she had secreted in the pocket of her nightdress.

"It's me. Doris. Are you all right?"

"Of course I am," answered Beryl. She took her hand off her knife. "What could hurt me out here?"

"Oh Beryl. You shouldn't just leave like that—if Miss Seccombe does a bed check, you'll get into trouble."

"So will you." Beryl looked at Doris warily. "Why are you out here?"

"I was worried about you."

Beryl nodded and, to her surprise, tears swam in her eyes.

Doris couldn't see the tears in the dark. She went on, "Mary is an absolute witch. I could have told her that a little sand boa wouldn't scare you, but she was so sure you would scream."

"What's she doing now?" Beryl asked slyly.

Doris clasped her hand over her mouth to keep back her giggles. "She's washing her hands like mad. None of the other girls will come near her. She's in hysterics."

Beryl and Doris laughed quietly together.

"Doris," Beryl began.

"Call me Dos," Doris interrupted. "All my friends do."

Warmth spread through Beryl. "Dos, why do they hate me?"

"They don't hate you. They don't understand you. Or what it's like to live in the bush. They all come from the city."

"But you understand, don't you?" Without knowing how, Beryl was certain that Dos had lived someplace wild.

Dos nodded. "My father has a farm out by Thika. My mother and I joined him two years ago. I loved it out there. Coming here felt like going to jail."

"Even my skin feels different here," Beryl said. "I don't know how I can last a whole year!"

Dos grabbed Beryl's hand. After a moment's hesitation, Beryl squeezed it back and said, "But you look like them. You talk like them. Dos, how do you do it?"

"My mother insisted that I be ladylike. She said someday I would go back to England, and she didn't want me to shock society. What about your mother?"

"I don't have one. Not really." In the darkness, Beryl could feel Dos' questioning look. "She's in England. She left when I was little."

"Oh."

"Can you help me?" The unfamiliar words felt strange on Beryl's tongue. "I promised my father I would go to school for a year, but I'm not sure I can last. If I get expelled, he'll send me to England. Tell me how to get along here."

Dos leaned back against a tree trunk to think. Finally she said, "Your main problem is Mary. She's used to bossing everybody around. Take care of her, and the others will go where they're led."

"I don't want to lead them!" Beryl cried. "Let Mary do that."

"You don't have a choice. Either lead them, or keep finding who knows what in your bed."

Beryl nodded. She would use her Nandi skills. She would watch carefully and study the enemy. Then she would make her move.

I made it to North America. Not quite as far as New York, but at the moment, I'm quite happy to be on terra firma. I lift my foot out of the bog and it squelches. I could have used some more firming in my terra. I breathe deeply and savor the silence and fresh air.

Now, to more practical matters. How am I to get out of here? A quick glance tells me that my poor old Messenger won't be flying me out. The propeller is buried in mud, and the engine has been ripped from the chassis. I feel much the same way.

No one knows to look for me, much less where. I'll have to rescue myself. It won't be the first time.

Easier said than done. I must have covered three miles, up to my waist in this nasty bog. The gash on my head has started to bleed again. Finally, I see a fisherman. He stares at me as though I'm that monster they found in Loch Ness.

"I'm Beryl Markham," I say. "I've just flown in from England."

He takes me to a godforsaken hut on a deserted stretch of coast. To my delight, there's a telephone. I turn to ask how a phone came to be there, but the fisherman answers first. "To report shipwrecks. You're the first plane crash."

I'm not one for looking in a mirror, but I suspect the expression on my face can best be described as rueful.

Within a day, I've been cleaned up and supplied with new clothes. There's a dashing bandage across my forehead. I'll have another scar to add to my collection. A plane, a Beechcraft, comes to collect me. The pilot lets me take a turn at the controls. To my relief, he doesn't say anything about the last plane I flew. I'm heading to New York City, where I'm told a crowd of well-wishers has been waiting for over a day. I'm being hailed as a great success.

Ha! If I had been successful, I'd be flying <u>The Messenger</u> out of here, instead of leaving her behind in a cold bog. At least I didn't drown. I'm one up on Icarus.

CHAPTER TWENTY-TWO

FOR THE NEXT WEEK, BERYL KEPT TO HERSELF AS SHE WATCHED the other students. Her first mistake, she decided, was trying to impress them at all. With the exception of Dos, she had never had any luck with girls. Everything she had ever learned from the Nandi was about being the best among the boys. She would start there.

She walked up to Sonny Bumpus on the makeshift cricket field marked with chalk lines. He was the most popular boy at school.

"I want to play, too," she said. Her words fell like coconuts from the palm trees—with a thud. The last time she had heard such deafening silence was the day she asked Arap Maina to let her hunt lion.

"No," Sonny said flatly. He was dressed in clothes that were slightly too small, and his pale complexion was pink and peeling from the sun. "You're a girl."

"I can bowl and hit as well as you can," Beryl insisted.

"Not likely." The other boys had gathered round. They laughed and congratulated Sonny as though he had said something clever.

Beryl took a deep breath. "If I can bowl, can I play?"

Sonny stared at her, then around the circle of boys. With their tacit approval, he said, "If you can stand at one end of the pitch and knock the bails off the other wicket, you can play."

The boys nudged each other and whispered excitedly. Beryl could guess what they were saying—the distance between the wickets was more than twenty yards. But Beryl had not learned to throw a spear at a moving animal for nothing. A wicket that stayed in one place and couldn't think for itself was an easy target.

"It's a bet," she said.

Beryl took up a bowling position at the wicket. She squinted into the sun to judge the distance to the other end of the field. Beryl tried to wiggle her toes in her tight shoes. It would be easier if she were barefoot, but she didn't think the boys would wait for her to unlace them.

The boys stood on the edge of the field, making rude comments.

"I bet she'll bend her elbow!"

"Who does she think she is? Jack Hobbs?"

And most infuriating of all, "Girls can't play cricket."

Beryl took the ball Sonny handed her. She examined it closely. Arap Maina had taught her to respect the special properties of a spear. Surely the ball deserved the same treatment. She weighed it in her hand, feeling the rough leather and the raised stitching. Holding the ball lightly by her fingertips, she swung her arm back in a windmill motion, without bending her elbow, and let it fly at the opposite wicket.

The ball sailed through the air and knocked off both bails on the distant wicket with a satisfying thump.

Beryl turned triumphantly to the boys as the ball bounced back toward the center of the pitch. "So, which team am I on?" she asked. Her smile faded when she saw the dismay in their faces.

Shoved forward by the others, Sonny spoke for all of them. "That didn't count. You—you . . . stepped outside the creases."

"I did no such thing!" Beryl narrowed her eyes and stomped over to him. "Sonny Bumpus, you made a deal. Are you welshing?"

There were few more insulting things to say to an Englishman, but to Beryl's mind, she had nothing to lose.

"Who are you calling a bloody Welshman?" Sonny said indignantly, his face turning brick red. But he wouldn't meet her accusing eyes. "You didn't do it right. How could you? Girls don't have the brain capacity to learn cricket." And with that, he turned his back to her.

"You can keep your stupid ball," she growled, throwing the ball into the dirt and walking away. Skip rope and cricket had been disastrous. It was time to play her own game.

Beryl waited for a day when it was raining too hard for outdoor recess. Finally, after a week, the moment was right. After Miss Seccombe left to take her tea, Beryl grabbed Dos by the arm. "Keep them here!" she whispered fiercely.

Puzzled but curious, Dos kept the other girls from leaving.

"What does she want now?" asked Mary.

"I don't know, but I'm not afraid to find out," Dos shot back. "Are you?"

Mary grimaced, but she stayed.

Beryl deliberately stood by the window, her tall figure framed by the gray light outside. "What do you know about steeple chasing?" she asked the group.

The girls murmured among themselves, confused.

"Isn't that when the horses jump the fences?" Doris asked.

"It's when the jockey races the horses over fences," corrected Beryl. "I do it all the time."

Mary couldn't stay silent. She strode over to confront Beryl. She stared into Beryl's blue eyes and accused, "You're lying again. Girls don't ride, and they don't race."

Beryl held onto her temper and said, "Girls ride on my father's farm. Or, at least, I do. I train the chasers for my father."

Mary drew in her breath, ready to denounce Beryl again, but Beryl interrupted, as though the idea had just occurred to her, "Why don't we do a steeplechase here?"

The girls looked at her blankly.

Dos began to giggle. "How? We have no horses."

"We race each other. We'll use the desks as fences." Beryl grabbed the nearest desk and started to drag it to the edge of the room.

"Why bother?" asked Mary. "It's so muggy." She twisted a limp curl around her finger.

"Is there anything better to do?" dared Beryl. No one had an answer to that. "Right then. Let's bring the next one over."

Caught up in Beryl's enthusiasm, Dos and the other girls began building a steeplechase course with ten desks around the edge of the classroom. One of the girls fetched the boys from their side of the school. Sonny Bumpus watched Beryl curiously, rocking back on his heels with his thumbs hitched in his trouser pockets.

Beryl stood in the center of the room and dictated the rules of the race. "Five times around will be the course. You must clear the desks. Touching the desk is all right, but if you knock over the inkwell, you're disqualified. Who'll be in the first heat?"

At first there were no takers. Beryl stared at each one of them, challenging them in the way Kibii had taught her. Finally, Sonny stepped forward and two other boys followed his lead.

"Excellent. Dos, you're the starting gun." Beryl hiked up her skirt so she could jump properly. The girls giggled at the sight of her knickers and the boys looked a little too closely, but Beryl didn't care.

"Ready, set, *go!*" shouted Dos.

The race began. Despite her tight shoes, as soon as Beryl began to leap the wide desks, her awkwardness melted away. Every part of her body worked perfectly. In a few seconds, the two other racers gave up to watch her.

Sonny did his best to keep up. He was a fast runner, but he couldn't jump as high as Beryl could. At the third desk, he knocked over an inkwell, spattering black ink across the whitewashed wall. Dos rushed to scrub the stain with her handkerchief.

Beryl ignored the mess and soared over the desks as though she were flying. After two circuits, Sonny finally gave up and stood gasping in the corner. Beryl ran with only one thought: to win. She did not notice she was the only one still racing.

Finally she came to a halt. The girls gaped at her and the boys shuffled their feet. "Did I win?" she asked, forcing herself to breathe through her nose. It wouldn't do to seem winded.

"Of course you did," said Dos. "How did you learn to jump like that?"

"The Nandi on our farm. They trained me to jump higher than my head. A desk is nothing."

"I don't believe you," Mary said scornfully. "You're lying again." And Sonny said, "Show us. I dare you."

"I beat you all at your own games, and mine, too. I don't need to prove anything else," Beryl cried.

"Of course, you would say that," said Mary spitefully, tossing her curls over her shoulder.

Beryl's back stiffened and her fists clenched by themselves. "Mary, if you call me a liar one more time, I'll . . ."

At that moment, Miss Seccombe returned. Her eyes darted from the rearranged desks, the ink spatter on the wall, and, worst of all, boys in the girls' classroom. "Boys, what are you doing in here?" she spluttered. "What's been going on?"

The room was silent.

"If no one answers, you will all lose recess."

Beryl pressed her lips tightly together and glared at the rest, daring them to tell.

"It was Beryl, Miss Seccombe," Mary said. "She wanted to do a steeplechase with the desks. I told her it was against the rules."

Beryl wanted to crush Mary's simpering face with her fist.

Miss Seccombe dismissed the other students, leaving Mary and Beryl standing in front of her. "Mary, thank you, dear, for your truthfulness. I know it's not easy to inform on a classmate."

She turned to Beryl. "Miss Clutterbuck, you will miss recess for one week. If there's another incident, you will not be permitted to be Alice in the play. Now clean up this mess." She walked out of the room.

Beryl marveled that Miss Seccombe, who understood her so little, could devise such a galling punishment. Being trapped inside for a week would be unbearable.

She glared at Mary. "I won't forget this, Mary Russell."

To her surprise, Mary was nearly in tears. "I can't understand it. I thought for sure she would take Alice away."

"You turned me in for a part in the stupid play?" Beryl asked incredulously.

"It's my part!" Mary cried.

"Alice is a sissy girl who doesn't have enough sense to get out of a bad dream." Beryl had finally read the book. She liked the shrinking and expanding, and thought the Cheshire Cat had possibilities, but she considered Alice a poor excuse for a heroine.

"She's a proper young lady. An English lady. She wears a pinafore and behaves herself. You could never play her!"

"Take the part—I don't care," Beryl protested.

"It's Miss Seccombe who decides—if she knew what a liar you were, she'd give Alice back to me."

Beryl had had enough. With her flat palm, she shoved Mary against the wall. "I have never lied," she growled. "Not once."

"Take your hands off me," said Mary.

"Not until you apologize."

Mary suddenly kicked Beryl in the shin with one of her pointy-toed boots.

Beryl's eyes watered with the pain. Without thinking, her right hand went to Mary's throat and started to squeeze. Mary gasped and swung her arms out wildly. She yanked a handful of Beryl's hair. A tangle of strands came away from the scalp. With her left hand, Beryl pulled up her skirt and grabbed the small dagger she now kept in the top of her stocking. She whipped it up under Mary's chin.

Mary began to cry.

Beryl glanced from Mary's scared face to the knife in her own hand. She heard Arap Maina's voice clearly in her head. "Beru, be kind to those who are afraid."

Not meeting Mary's eyes, Beryl stepped back and put away her knife. This was not the way to solve her problem with Mary. She walked to the window and said, "You are a stupid girl. But I won't stain my blade with your blood."

Now that there was some distance between them, Mary looked braver. Between her sobs, she cried, "You are a savage who doesn't belong here. The others may believe your lies, but I know better." She ran out howling.

Beryl sank down to the floor and held her head in her hands. How was it that Mary was the witch, but it was Beryl who felt ashamed?

A week later, they began rehearsing *Alice in Wonderland*. Beryl reluctantly put on her costume of a red dress covered with a white pinafore and tied a ribbon in her blond hair. Looking in the mirror in the dormitory, she had to admit she looked just like the illustrations in Mr. Carroll's book.

She tucked her latest letter from Arthur in the wide pocket of her skirt. It was short and contained many misspellings, but he wrote of horses and home. He was most excited about how high he could jump now. She smiled as she thought of him bouncing up and down.

Taking a last look at the demure stranger in the mirror, she laughed out loud. She was finished with good behavior. She was about to introduce the real Beryl to Miss Seccombe and the Nairobi School for European Children.

The children were assembled in the yard for a cast photo. As the tallest, Beryl stood in the back. Mary, who played the Red Queen, was seated on a low throne in front of her. Mary had primped for an hour to be ready. While the photographer readied his plates, Beryl was preparing, too.

"Stop fidgeting, Beryl," scolded Miss Seccombe.

"Everyone look at me," the photographer said. He held up a large magnesium flashbulb. There was a flash that left them all blinded.

"Miss Seccombe, that hurt my eyes," Mary complained.

"I'll take one more," the photographer said.

"Beryl, why can't you stand still?" Miss Seccombe asked peevishly.

"Sorry," Beryl muttered. Standing straight, she bent the other leg in front of her; her fingers busily unlaced her shoe.

Another flash and the photographer released them. The cast began to move away. Beryl straightened her shoulders, kicked her shoes off, and gathered herself for a giant leap. Like an eagle, she rose in the air and flew over Mary. Glancing behind her, she grinned at Mary's stunned face.

She landed in front of the class. Everyone stared at her. She began to leap in place. Hopping, then levitating. No longer imprisoned in the ill-fitting shoes, her feet in white stockings felt like tiny wings propelling her higher. Her skirt swirled around her, and the pinafore floated up like a cloud. Higher and still higher. If she tried just a little harder, she could fly.

Dos clapped her hands in delight. "She's jumping higher than her head. I knew she could."

Sonny's face showed a reluctant respect. Mary sulked in the back of the crowd.

Beryl stopped suddenly and glared at everyone standing in the circle around her. "So there," she said.

Mrs. Seccombe's nasal voice broke the silence. "Beryl Clutterbuck, what exactly do you think you are doing? This is no place for ballet leaps."

Beryl could see it in the others' faces; they understood it was not ballet. It was the training that a young Nandi received to become a warrior, just as Beryl had claimed. From that moment, Beryl would always have the upper hand with Mary.

Now I know how Alice felt stepping through that looking glass.

When we land in New York, five thousand people are waiting to see me! I don't know that I've ever seen so many people at one time. At first I can't make out what they are chanting. Then I realize these odd New Yorkers are saying, "Hello, Blondie!"

I put my arms above my head and bow deeply from the waist. "Salaam!" I shout.

The crowd goes wild.

Amidst the deafening sound of thousands of car horns hooting, I am escorted by a troop of police motorcycles to the Ritz-Carlton. The next day, I go to the mayor's reception. Mayor La Guardia is a rumpled little man. I tower over him. He is sweating and mopping his forehead with his handkerchief.

"Hot, isn't it?" he says.

I agree politely, but honestly, I grew up in Africa!

There's a stack of telegrams and tributes from the newspapers. From Peru, my father said, "Beryl's a grand girl. I knew she would triumph, but in spite of my faith in her abilities, yesterday was the most anxious day I have known."

There was even an interview with my mother, who has—irony of ironies—returned to Nairobi. She said she never had any doubts that I would do it. "My daughter," she said, "has always been extremely self-confident and full of pluck from the time she was a tiny tot." I wonder what the papers would say if I told them I barely know her?

Amelia Earhart said she was "delighted beyond words that Mrs. Markham should have succeeded in her exploit."

And Tom Black? Dear Tom, the master of under-statement. He said, "Amazing! I thought she'd do it, but the weather, on what is always a tough crossing, seemed appallingly bad."

I'm not sentimental as a rule, but I think I might keep these scraps of paper forever.

CHAPTER TWENTY-THREE

CHATTERING LIKE MACAWS, MISS SECCOMBE'S CLASS ENTERED
the foyer of the New Stanley Hotel. All the British settlers preferred
to stay here in Nairobi's finest hotel. Beryl glanced around at the tall
columns and the marble expanse of the lobby, familiar to her from
visits with her father. Miss Seccombe arranged the annual outing
as an opportunity for the girls to practice their social skills at a very
ladylike tea.

Beryl drew Dos to one side. "Dos, my head itches!" she whispered,
picking at her mane, which had been tamed into a demure bun.

"I told you to wash your hair last night." Dos elbowed her hard.
"Beryl, I've been looking forward to this for weeks. If you make a
scene, I'll . . . I'll tell Sonny Bumpus you like him!"

"That shrimp? I don't think so."

"Then behave!"

Miss Seccombe beckoned the girls to follow her into the dining
room, where three tables were waiting for them. Beryl hung back,

knowing she wouldn't be missed for a few minutes. She slipped into the dark lounge, which was filled with men smoking cigars. The smell of fine whiskey permeated even the upholstered furniture. Reminded of her father's office, Beryl smiled.

She walked to the bar and slapped the counter like her father did on their visits to Nairobi. The barkeep looked around and behind her, searching for her chaperone.

"You don't belong in here, young lady," he said.

"Don't you recognize me?" she asked. "I haven't been here for a long time, but you used to give me fizzy lemonades."

The bartender looked closer. Then his face lightened and he smiled broadly. "If it isn't Captain Clutt's daughter!" His eyes darted around the room. "Where's the Captain?"

"I'm here on my own," Beryl confided. "I'm supposed to be in the dining room on a school trip."

He winked. "Your secret is safe with me. What can I get you?"

"Do you have a newspaper I can look at?"

"Certainly." He pulled out a much-read paper from under the bar. Then he poured her a glass of fizzy lemonade. "On the house," he said.

Beryl thanked him, sat down on a barstool, and opened the sporting pages. The headline read, "Night Hawk Wins the St. Leger Stakes."

"The St. Leger? But that's run in mid-September," Beryl said. The racing calendar in England and Nairobi was the only calendar she ever cared about.

"Every year," the barkeep agreed. "Night Hawk was the odds-on favorite."

"So the race ran already?" Beryl asked. "What day is it?"

The bartender laughed. "It's the sixteenth. I guess they don't teach you about horse racing at that school of yours."

Beryl gulped down her sweet drink, said good-bye, and raced out of the lounge into the dining room. Her abrupt arrival drew everyone's eyes. The girls from the school group were sitting at their tables in the corner. Miss Seccombe was nowhere to be seen. Beryl rushed over to Dos.

"Where did you go?" Dos asked. "Miss Seccombe just went looking for you."

Beryl shrugged. "Let her. It's my independence day!"

"What are you talking about?"

"Actually, it's two days past independence day! My year was up the day before yesterday. It's time for me to go home." Beryl laughed at herself. "I was so busy trying not to think about how long I had to wait, I lost track of the date!"

"You're leaving now?"

The other girls hung on Beryl's every word.

"There's not a moment to waste! The train station is just up the street, right?"

Dos nodded, but her face was full of concern. "You can't just leave! Shouldn't you wait for your father to come get you?"

"Ha!" Beryl exclaimed, silencing their corner of the busy dining room. "He wouldn't bother. He knows that I'll get home on my own. It's been grand getting to know you. Come visit any time! Good-bye!"

She turned to leave, but Dos grabbed her wrist. "What about your things?" she asked.

"Keep them! Who wants all those scratchy dresses and tight shoes?" Beryl said happily. Then a thought struck her. "But there is one thing . . ."

"What?" Then Dos remembered the only possession that Beryl cared about. "The lion's paw."

"I have to go back to school to get it." Beryl looked through her battered purse for change to pay for a rickshaw. "Oh, bother. I don't have enough money. Can I borrow some?"

"I won't let you take a rickshaw by yourself," Dos said. "I'll come, too."

Beryl was unpinning her bun. She shook out her braids. "Dos, I've hunted lions and warthogs. I don't need an escort."

"I insist," Dos said.

"Won't you get in trouble?"

Grinning, Dos shook her head. "Not with you to blame, I won't!"

Beryl shrugged. "Suit yourself. We'd better go before Miss Seccombe comes back."

"Wait for us," one of the other girls said.

"I don't want to be here when Miss Seccombe realizes that Beryl has done it again!" said another.

Before Beryl could protest, the entire class, with the exception of Mary Russell, followed her out of the dining room. Glancing behind her, Beryl couldn't help but compare the colorful procession of girls in fancy dresses wielding purses and parasols to a parade of Nandi warriors. Outside in the street, she commandeered enough rickshaws to carry them all back to the Nairobi School for European Children.

Dos sat with Beryl as their driver panted up the hill. "Mary must be having a fit," Dos giggled. "I'm sure she's told Miss Seccombe everything by now. They won't be far behind us."

"Let them!" Beryl said. "I won't take long."

The seven girls clattered up the wooden stairs and brushed past the confused servant who opened the front door. They hauled out Beryl's trunk and began to pack it for her. Beryl grabbed her rucksack and went to Miss Seccombe's office. The headmistress kept all the contraband locked in a desk drawer. Beryl wasted no time; she forced the lock with her knife. She burrowed through the confiscated items: liqueur-filled candy, love letters, and Parisian fashion magazines. Finally she found a cloth bundle she recognized. The paw! She tucked it away carefully in her rucksack.

As she returned to the dormitory, she stopped short. Miss Seccombe stood in the doorway, her face flushed and angry. Mary hovered behind her. The rest of the girls were standing against the wall as though they were facing a firing squad. Only Dos would meet Beryl's eye; she winked.

"Beryl Clutterbuck, this is the last straw!" Miss Seccombe cried. "When I found the girls were gone, I knew it was you, even before Mary told me. Ever since you arrived, you've been nothing but trouble." She extended one bony finger in blame. "It was you who backed up the drains! And set fire to the rubbish dump. And don't deny that you put the beetles in my washbasin."

"Yes, that's right." With her sentence up, Beryl had nothing to lose.

"If you think I'll tolerate this sort of behavior at my school, you are sadly—"

"I quit!" Beryl interrupted.

"You are in my care. You cannot quit."

Beryl stared at Miss Seccombe without troubling to conceal her loathing. "I'm leaving on the afternoon train, and you can't stop me."

"I shall, even if I have to physically restrain you!" Miss Seccombe slapped Beryl across the face. Dos and Beryl's other friends gasped. Mary stepped back, out of reach.

Beryl stood motionless. She touched her cheek. Then, as though her hand had a mind of its own, her fingers found the back of Miss Seccombe's cotton dress. She lifted the headmistress a few inches off the ground and shook her hard, like a terrier shaking a rat. Miss Seccombe's tight hair came undone in bunches. When Beryl dropped her, she sank to the ground.

As if a mouse was squeaking, Beryl heard Miss Seccombe's voice repeating, "You're expelled. You're expelled."

"You can't expel me; I've already quit," shouted Beryl. "Goodbye, Dos!" Abandoning every possession except her rucksack, Beryl stalked out and headed for the train station.

Beryl was alone on the train whose whistle had haunted her dreams for the past year. With a sharp, metallic jerk, it began the climb out of Nairobi toward the highlands.

Pressing her face against the smeared glass, Beryl stared out at the dusty plains rolling slowly by. Giraffes and herds of antelope were visible in the distance. A rough hand on her shoulder startled her. She banged her forehead on the glass. She whirled to see the conductor, Nelson. As long as she could remember, he had patrolled the length of the train with his rolling gait.

He pushed his face down toward hers and in a hoarse voice he asked, "So, where's your father, Miss Beryl?" His voice rasped from decades of escorting the dusty and smoky train.

"I'm to meet him in Nakuru. But it's fine, Nelson; he'll pay for my return ticket," Beryl said, leaning back, away from his tobacco and whiskey breath.

"Oh we don't worry about tickets overmuch with our old friends," he said. "School's not out yet, is it?"

"Not exactly, I'm . . . I'm just . . ."

"Running away, are you?" he asked with a knowing grin.

"Oh, no," Beryl reassured him virtuously. "I tried that before, but they knew I would go for the train and they caught me at the station. This time, I was expelled."

Nelson burst out laughing. The sound traveled up and down the car, causing the other passengers to look up to hear the joke. "Your father will have something to say about that. The Captain doesn't tolerate people who go against his plans. I remember that time the lad watered the horses too much on the journey down. Unfit to race, they were. I thought the Captain was going to thrash him right there in the horse car."

"He'll understand," Beryl said. "I hope." She thought about the deal she had made with her father. With a shake of her head, she pulled down the window to look out, but she drew back when sparks flew by her face.

"Miss Beryl, if you are going to stick your head out, you had better wear these." Nelson handed her a set of goggles. "I'd wager those sparks are from your own father's forest. He supplies the railroad with the wood for the steam engines. We used to have to carry enough wood up to the highlands to make the return trip. But now we just pick it up from him at Nakuru."

The train began to climb a steep incline—not as steep as Beryl knew it would be later—and the engine whined in protest.

"That fool engineer didn't get enough speed to climb the hill. So we've . . . run out of steam."

Beryl chuckled politely, although she had heard Nelson's joke many times. She knew exactly what would happen next. The engineer would back up, let the engine cool, and try again.

With a shudder felt through the train, the engine began to reverse. With a relieved hiss, the train began slipping backward down the incline.

Nelson sat down beside her. "We'll be waiting for a bit. Did I ever tell you about how I helped build the Lunatic Express?"

"Lunatic Express?" Beryl had heard the train called many things, most of them uncomplimentary, but never that.

"That's what they called this train. To settle British East Africa, the Crown sold the land cheap. Folks like Lord Delamere and your father were the first to come up. But they needed the train to take their crops back down. The line cost millions of pounds and the lives of hundreds of men."

As long as Beryl could remember, the train to Nairobi had been a fact of life—as much taken for granted as the rains in spring. Without it, there were no settlements. She wondered what would Africa be like without the British. If you soared over it like a bird, there would be no roads, no ugly scars of train tracks, no gas-powered lights to cloud the sky and block the stars. Arap Maina probably remembered how it was. But that would be an Africa that had no place for Beryl Clutterbuck.

"How did you build it?" asked Beryl.

"With British ingenuity," Nelson chuckled. "The engineers were from home, but we imported the labor from India. I was a young man then." He sighed. Looking at his potbelly and thinning hair, Beryl found it difficult to believe he had ever been young. "Aye, I was a junior assistant surveyor. We would set up camp ahead of the line and then build the track behind us. Those were the days. If only the lions had left us alone."

The images of Arap Maina's clawed chest and her punctured leg rose in her mind.

The train reached a plateau and slowly came to a halt.

"Well, lass, that's our cue. Do you want to step outside? We'll be here for a bit while the engine cools down."

Beryl followed the other passengers off the train. They had been traveling for only a few hours, but everyone was already sore and dusty from the journey. As she stretched, a movement in the distance caught her eye. "Is that a lion?"

"You've good eyes," Nelson said with approval. "Like I was telling you—lions were a terrible problem when we were laying this track. They would hunt in pairs. More than one man was pulled from his bed. After a while, they stopped eating the men—just killed 'em for the sport."

"I've never heard of lions doing that," said Beryl, her forehead crinkled in disbelief.

"I swear it's true, Miss Beryl; those lions were fierce. They out-numbered us. We paid dearly for every mile of track."

When the train finally started again, Beryl boarded in a thoughtful mood, considering for the first time the price her father and other settlers had paid for the right to settle in the highlands.

The train made its way upward. It was late morning when it finally gasped its way into Nakuru.

"Good-bye, Nelson, and thank you," said Beryl as she hopped off the train before it even stopped.

"Miss Beryl, don't you have any luggage?" he called after her.

"Don't worry," she shouted as she ran out of the car. "Have a good journey back." She ran out of the station to prevent any more awkward questions.

As soon as she was out of sight, she began stripping off the awful clothes. The shoes were the first to go. Then the stockings. She sliced off the bottom of the full blue cotton skirt with her knife and wrapped it lengthwise around her body, securing it with a knot at her shoulder like a *shuka*. Her blouse and hat she left on the track for anyone foolish enough to want them. Her bare feet protesting at the unaccustomed sensation of stones and dirt, she ran all the way to the Nandi village.

The dogs and children greeted her joyfully, but she did not stop to talk. She wanted to see Kibii and Arap Maina. Arap Maina appeared at the doorway to his hut, smiling at the sight of her.

"I'm back, Arap Maina!" she announced. She wanted to hug him, but she knew his dignity would not permit it. She forced her arms to stay at her sides, contenting herself with a huge grin.

"Beru, welcome. Your father thought you would be back a few days ago."

"I should have been," Beryl said. She tried to look past Arap Maina into the hut. "Where is Kibii?" She had not seen her friend since he had left for his circumcision ritual, although she had thought of him often.

"Kibii is no more," he said solemnly.

Beryl caught her breath, "You mean . . ."

"He is now Arap Ruta," said Arap Maina with pride.

Relieved, Beryl nodded. Kibii was not dead; he had become a *murani*. His new name meant that he had passed his ritual and was now a man.

"I hoped he would be back by now," said Beryl, hardly trying to conceal her disappointment.

"Beru, the warriors live by themselves in a separate camp. It is how they develop the bonds of brothers. He has taken his proper place with the tribe. It is what he was born to do."

Blinking against the sudden tears in her eyes, Beryl started to turn away. Arap Maina touched her shoulder and said gently, "You have grown tall and strong while you were away. It is time for you to join your own people. Go home."

"But this is my home, too," protested Beryl.

"We shall always be friends. But you are the daughter of Cluttabucki, and he has plans for you. Go see him. Go now. It will not be as hard as you think." Arap Maina disappeared into his hut.

Beryl trekked up the hill to the farm, thinking hard. Trapped in Nairobi, she had dreamed of the Nandi. And now the Nandi told her she belonged with the British. Was it truly time to choose?

I'm wearing a couture gown, hiking up the long skirt to climb the stairs to yet another banquet in my honor. They are getting dull.

Blast, there's another reporter. He's from <u>The New York Times</u>, I think. He's seen me, too—no avoiding another impertinent interview now. I paste on my broadest smile.

"Beryl, do you have any comment about Tom Black's death?"

I feel as though I've received a blow to the gut, but I don't show it. "Excuse me?"

The reporter delights in telling me the whole story.

It was a million-to-one accident. My dear Tom was taxiing down the runway in a new plane, a tiny Percival

Mew. I've heard about this plane. A hairy little beast to fly, but fast. It's only four feet tall when it's on the ground. The bomber pilot didn't even see it when he came in for a landing. The bomber's propeller sliced through its cockpit, and Tom, too, like a knife through butter. He died half an hour later. All his skill and experience counted for nothing. I can hardly believe it's true.

Choking on my grief, I give the reporter what he wants. "England has lost a wonderful pilot," I say. "And I have lost the instructor who taught me all I know about flying."

I cancel the rest of my engagements and book passage on the first ship back to England.

CHAPTER TWENTY-FOUR

BERYL WALKED HOME THE LONG WAY, ALONG THE EDGE OF THE forest. She stopped and peered up into the cedar trees. Through the beards of lichen dripping from the branches, she glimpsed birds swooping among the leaves. She inhaled and exhaled sharply, trying to get the brackish air of the Nairobi swamps out of her lungs.

The forest ended sooner than she remembered. Her father had been busy, taming the forest, turning it into profit. Buller was lying in the dirt as though he had been waiting patiently for a year.

"Hi, boy," she said, fondling his scarred ears and rubbing under his chin. His tail thumped, and with a wheezing noise he stood and followed her down to the lower paddock.

As she hoped, her father was putting the Baron through his paces. If he was not too busy, the Captain loved to ride after the day's work was done.

Beryl walked into the paddock, her chin up, head held high. She was uneasily conscious of her makeshift *shuka*—who ever heard of a toga made out of a skirt? The Captain saw her, reined in the Baron, and waited for her to close the distance between them. Horse and master were silhouetted against the setting sun. Thankfully, Emma was nowhere to be seen.

Beryl's stomach fluttered as though she had swallowed a nest of wasps. But despite her nerves, she couldn't help savoring the feel of the damp, packed earth of the paddock under her bare feet. As she placed each step, she rolled from heel to toe. It was a stretch that reminded her feet of all the liberties they had once known. She told herself to agree to anything her father proposed—anything to keep her feet out of those dreadful shoes.

Finally there was no more space between them. The Captain's face was impassive. The Baron chomped noisily on his bit. Now that she was here, all her words, so carefully planned on the train, deserted her.

"Beryl," the Captain said noncommittally.

"Daddy." She tried to show him her resolve without looking defiant.

"You lasted longer than I thought you would."

"We agreed on a year. I lasted a year and two days," she said.

Looking down from his horse, the Captain's gray eyes challenged her to be more truthful.

"I did run away earlier, but they caught me at the station."

He leaned forward interrogatively.

"Twice," she admitted.

"I know; the headmistress wrote to Emma." His eyes narrowed, and his hand tightened on his reins. "And now? Are you absent without leave?" The military term came easily to his lips.

"Oh no, Daddy," Beryl assured him. "I was expelled." After a moment, she added doubtfully, "Honorably expelled."

His hands lost some of their tension and he nodded. "Yes, I thought you might be."

"Well, really I quit a moment before that awful woman threw me out."

Captain Clutterbuck burst out laughing.

Taking a deep breath and placing all her hopes in her voice, Beryl implored, "Daddy, don't make me go back. I hated it!"

"I didn't send you to enjoy yourself. I sent you to get an education." He paused; he was as honest as his daughter. "And to get you out of harm's way."

"It's a lot more dangerous down there. You have no idea how complicated the other girls were."

He chuckled. "Oh, my dear, I've known for many years how complicated girls can be."

"But I've grown up a lot . . ." she paused. "Can I come back if I promise to behave with Emma?"

"Just with Emma?" His eyes were twinkling.

Beryl's nervousness began to fade. "Definitely with her, and I'll try to behave the rest of the time."

He waited.

"I'll try hard."

Suddenly the Captain relaxed, too. He dismounted smoothly and enveloped her in a large hug. "Darling, I've missed you. It's been dull without you here!"

Beryl said nothing, too busy savoring his unexpected welcome. Her father put his strong hands on her shoulders and pushed her back a step. Her eyes were level with his.

"Let me look at you. You've grown at least two hands."

"I'm not a horse," she protested happily.

He chuckled.

"So I can come home?"

"If you agree to my conditions . . ."

She began to nod eagerly, but in a burst of caution she asked, "What do you have in mind?"

"No more larking about with Kibii," he said.

"That won't be hard—he's a warrior now. He doesn't want anything to do with me," she said sadly.

"So Kibii is growing up, is he? Good. So will you."

She watched him warily, shifting from one bare foot to the other.

"I'm expanding the farm all the time. I can't run the stables without a head lad. Are you interested in the job?"

"You want me to be head lad?" She couldn't keep the hopeful disbelief out of her voice.

"Can you do it?" he asked. His voice was that of a commanding officer offering an ensign a vital assignment in wartime. Beryl remembered he had used the same tone when he suggested she ride Camiscan for the first time.

"Of course I can!" Suddenly her future looked brighter.

"And you can't live in that *rondavel*. That back wall isn't safe."

"I have to live with you and Emma?"

"I've got something else in mind." He pointed across the paddock, up the hill to the house. Next to his house stood a new house. An adorable cottage with gables and three windows. Even from here, she could see it was twice the size of her *rondavel* and had at least two rooms. There were even proper shingles, not thatch, for a roof.

"Do you like it?" he asked, smiling.

"It's for me?"

"For you," he confirmed. "Emma insisted that if you are to have a proper job with me, you need a proper home." He grinned. "But not under her roof."

Beryl remembered the catty remarks she had heard from Margaret, and how rude Miss Seccombe had been to Emma. Her position, neither wife nor housekeeper, was a difficult one.

"She must be lonely," Beryl said. "Perhaps I should be nicer."

A quizzical look appeared on her father's face. "What did they do to you at that school?"

"I lived with seven other girls for a year, Daddy."

"Enough said," he laughed. "If you and Emma could declare a truce, my life would be easier."

"A job with the horses. My own house. No hunting. Stop tormenting Emma. Is that all?"

A bit of his stern manner returned. "And for God's sake, put on some decent clothes!"

"Agreed!" Beryl gave her father another hug. His arm draped around her shoulder, they began walking toward the stable.

Beryl knew that her father would not retract his offer, so it was safe to ask. "Daddy, why now? You said before I couldn't work in the stable."

"The most practical reason is that the school costs a fortune for an education you don't need." His voice was rueful. "After all, I can't see you going to university in England."

Beryl nodded.

"Secondly, I'm so busy with the mill, I need someone to keep an eye on the stable. I have almost one hundred thoroughbreds here—

the whole bloodstock of British East Africa. Finally, you want the job, and I want you to be happy."

Beryl would have preferred her happiness be at the top of his list, but she wouldn't complain about the result.

"So it's time to put you to work," the Captain said, returning to his usual brisk style. "Do you remember Coquette?"

"Daddy, I went away to school, not the moon. Of course I remember! The golden Abyssinian mare with a white mane."

"She's due to foal soon."

"Who's the stud? Camiscan?"

"No, a new stallion, Referee. It promises to be a good foal." He paused. "Coquette is your responsibility."

Beryl felt lightheaded. "Daddy, I've never birthed a foal."

"Coquette has never had a foal either. First things aren't always easy. You both will learn."

Ten long days later, Coquette was finally ready. Beryl was alone in the stall with her and stroked the mare's nose with pity. Coquette's golden coat was tarnished and her eyes were dull. She was so full of new life that it had sucked her own vitality out of her.

"You will be beautiful again," Beryl said to her. "As soon as this is finished."

A hurricane lamp burned on its hook in the corner, well away from the straw.

"Why are foals always born in the middle of the night?" Emma's voice startled Beryl. She whirled around to see Emma holding a plate covered with a cloth.

"I don't know," Beryl admitted. "But they always are."

"I brought you something to eat," Emma said.

"Thank you." Beryl turned back to Coquette.

"Beryl, I know we haven't always got along, but I wanted to tell you how happy I am that you are home. Your father missed you very much."

Beryl was silent, and after a few moments, she heard Emma's footsteps moving off.

Coquette made a groaning noise. Her labor had started. Beryl whistled for the stable lad who would help her. To her surprise, Arthur—not so little now—came running.

"What are you doing here?" she asked, not taking her eyes from Coquette.

"Dad thought I should watch."

"Get the kit," she ordered.

He came back at a run with her foaling bag, which contained knives, twine, disinfectant, and even anesthetic. Beryl could not help the mare yet, but she could keep her company. Arthur sat in the corner and watched, his eyes wide.

After what felt like hours, Coquette's eyes seemed a little brighter; it was time. Beryl knelt beside her, waiting for the first glimpse of the foal in its sac. She could see the tiny hooves; the foal's legs were gathered together to ease its way into the world. Gently, Beryl pulled as Coquette pushed. The nose, the head, and at last the whole foal slipped out of Coquette and into Beryl's arms.

Arthur handed Beryl her knife, and she slit open the birth sac. The foal's tiny nostrils sucked air for the first time. Beryl pulled the sac away from its body and cut the cord. She bathed the cord with disinfectant. She saw now that the foal was a colt.

Coquette lurched to her feet and with listless eyes looked down on her son. She and Beryl washed him together; Coquette with her long tongue, Beryl with a towel.

Beryl heard a cough behind her and turned to see her father. The proud look on his face was the only thing that could top the night's triumph.

"Well done," he said.

"Beryl did a great job, didn't she, Dad?" Arthur chimed in.

"She did. He's a fine colt. Shall I reward you or Coquette— or both?"

"It was Coquette who did all the work," Beryl said.

"Ah, but it's you who'll get the reward. You brought him into the world; he's yours," her father said.

"Wow!" Arthur exclaimed. "Beryl, the next time you run away you can ride."

"I won't be leaving again," Beryl assured them. "Everything I want is here."

After Beryl and Arthur had cleaned up the foaling box, she left him to watch over the mother and newborn. Beryl sat against the wall of her new house, looking up at the bright stars in the sky.

After a time, she heard the faint sounds of someone approaching from the forest. She smiled to herself and waited until the near-silent figure approached her cottage.

"Hello, Kibii," she said in Swahili.

He was very solemn, and in the bright starlight, Beryl could see that he was feeling very full of himself. The Nandi made such a fuss of new warriors that it was hard not to get a swelled head. Kibii's skull was freshly shaved, and she could see the ochre paint in intricate designs on his body.

"Yes, Beru, it is I."

"But you are no longer Kibii."

"I am Arap Ruta," he said with pride. The "R" sound came out as smooth and soft as feathers on the lips. "I am a *murani* now," he said simply.

"Congratulations," she said solemnly.

He asked curiously, "Why are you looking up so seriously? What is there to see but sky?"

"When I was in Nairobi, I thought the stars were different there. But it is the same sky. It was me who was different. Now that I am back, I see that the constellations did not change. Maybe it is the same sky everywhere? Maybe even in London?"

"We are not birds or bats to worry about the sky."

"But think of it—if you were a bird, you could go from one place to another without using roads, railroad tickets, or papers. It wouldn't matter if you were from Africa or Europe."

"Or if you were a white girl or I a Nandi warrior?"

"Exactly!"

"Beru, my father always said you had clouds in your eyes."

They were silent as they contemplated the night sky. Beryl wondered what it was about talking under the stars that made you feel so solemn and wise.

Kibii broke the silence. "I hear the mare birthed a fine colt."

"Yes. My father gave him to me."

"What will you name him?"

"That is why I was looking up at the sky. I was trying to think of the perfect name. I was thinking, perhaps Pegasus."

"Peg-a-sus?" Kibii could not get his tongue around the unfamiliar name.

"He is a winged horse out of one of our stories. A winged horse that heroes rode."

"Like the cans of paraffin?"

Beryl laughed out loud as she realized that Kibii was right. The fuel cans that all the settlers used had a winged red horse emblazoned on the side with the motto "Pegasus, the spirit of mileage and power."

She giggled. "Yes, like the fuel cans."

"It's a good name," conceded Kibii.

"So is yours, Arap Ruta."

"I came to say good-bye."

"I know." Beryl's heart was full with many emotions. She grieved for the loss of Kibii, but she was happy for Arap Ruta.

"Good-bye for now? Or forever?" she asked.

For a moment, she glimpsed Kibii in the eyes of the dignified Arap Ruta. "For now, I owe my life to the tribe."

"And I must help my father."

"Someday, we will be friends again," he said, and melted away quicker than he had come.

"It's a promise," she whispered after him into the night.

A NOTE TO THE READER

You might be wondering how much of *Promise the Night* is true. The answer is, most of the good parts! The rest is my imagination.

Beryl Clutterbuck was born in 1902 in England. At the age of two, she accompanied her parents and her older brother, Richard, to the new colony of British East Africa, now known as Kenya. Her father, Captain Charles Clutterbuck, was a distinguished horseman turned farmer, trainer, and miller. He settled in the highlands above Nairobi. His farm, Green Hills, overlooked the Rift Valley, one of the great sights of Kenya.

Like most of the British colonists, the family initially lived in a *rondavel*, a hut made of mud and daub with a thatch roof. The conditions were difficult and primitive and proved too rigorous for his wife, Clara, who had been a socialite with a reputation for riding well in fox hunts. She abandoned her husband and daughter to return to England with Beryl's brother. She left with a British officer she met in Nairobi, who was having his wooden teeth seen to by a dentist. Beryl did not see her mother or brother again until she was an adult. Clara left behind a dog, Buller, who did get snatched by a leopard from Beryl's hut. He survived, but was never quite the same afterward.

Beryl spent her early years cared for by members of the Nandi tribe who worked for her father. She was accepted as an honorary member of the tribe. Her best friend was a boy named Kibii, and together they trained to be warriors in the Nandi way. Their teacher was his father, Arap Maina, who also worked for Beryl's father.

Beryl participated in many hunts. She wrote about them in her memoir, *West Into the Night,* and in other short stories published in various magazines. Arap Maina was conscripted by the British forces to fight in World War I against the Germans. He was killed almost instantly. Beryl and Kibii were both very bitter about the senselessness of his death.

The British ladies in the highlands often remonstrated with the Captain about his only daughter being raised by a native tribe. He tried to remedy this situation by installing Emma Orchardson as his housekeeper. She had a son, Arthur, and a husband who was more interested in his research of native rituals than in his family. Emma was very pretty and vivacious. Perhaps inevitably, the Captain and Emma grew closer. Beryl resented their relationship very deeply. By all reports, Emma was never anything but kind to Beryl, but Beryl always hated her.

Because of Emma's relationship with the Captain, she and, by extension, Green Hills Farm, were ostracized by the other English settlers. This left Beryl isolated from colonial society and other girls her age.

Miss Le May was a real person who did beat Beryl mercilessly. Beryl ran away for several weeks and stayed in a cave and hid with the Nandi before she finally tricked Miss Le May into abusing Beryl within earshot of her father.

It is also true that Beryl was mauled by a tame lion named Paddy. He spent the rest of his life in a cage until he was executed when the Elkingtons could no longer keep him. Beryl describes this incident in *West Into the Night*. In her own diaries, Margaret Elkington wrote that Beryl had exaggerated the seriousness of her wounds.

Beryl was sent to—and expelled from—not one boarding school but two. Although Arthur was also sent to boarding school with her, Beryl never referred to him in her memoir or her reminiscences. In *Promise the Night*, I combined the stories of students who knew her, including Sonny Bumpus, who became a lifelong friend and her chief jockey. The steeplechase race, the girls following Beryl home from a field trip, and the shaking of her teacher "as a terrier shakes a rat" are all documented anecdotes from her school years.

When Beryl returned from school the second time, her father gave up on her formal education. He built her a lovely house (that still stands today) and offered her a job running his stables. When she supervised the birth of a foal out of Coquette by Referee, he gave her the horse. She named him Pegasus.

At the age of eighteen, Beryl was abandoned by her remaining parent. The Captain was bankrupted by drought, and relocated to Peru. Beryl told him she could not leave Africa because she did not know it completely, and what she did know, she loved too well.

Beryl became a very successful trainer of horses. She won many of the most prestigious races in Nairobi, despite her youth and her gender—neither of which endeared her to the all-male racing establishment. Arthur stayed in Nairobi and was one of her best jockeys.

In her twenties, just when Beryl was feeling overwhelmed by her responsibilities as a trainer and businesswoman, her old friend,

Kibii, now known as Arap Ruta, re-entered her life and quickly became her head lad. But when airplanes arrived in Africa, she abandoned horses for flight. Arap Ruta was right behind her, learning to be her chief mechanic. She joked that he used to groom her planes. Tom Black was her first instructor and remained her mentor. There was a romantic relationship between them, but he eventually married another woman.

Beryl was one of the first women to receive a commercial pilot's license. For several years she made a living ferrying mail, medical patients, and supplies to the widespread settlements of East Africa. She even made a very good wage spotting elephants for the "Great White Hunters," who came to Africa to take home the enormous tusks.

In 1936, Beryl joined other world-famous aviators who were setting and breaking flight records. Lord Carberry dared her to make the flight from England to North America. The flight was considered particularly difficult because you flew into the night and the winds were against you. She crossed the Atlantic, but crash-landed on the coast of Cape Breton in Nova Scotia. She was transported to New York City to a triumphant welcome. Many of the details I include were inspired by Beryl's account of her voyage that the *Daily Express* paid her to send as soon as she arrived.

Years later, Beryl wrote a personal memoir called *West with the Night*. She had married and divorced an English lord, Gervase Markham, and wrote under her married name. *West with the Night* became a literary sensation and established her reputation as an adventuress. An early admirer was the renowned writer Ernest Hemingway.

After a brief stint advising on aviation for films in Hollywood, Beryl returned to Africa. She took up horse training again, and enjoyed the same success she had as a young woman. Her father eventually settled in South Africa. When he died in 1957, he was a successful trainer. He left his house and estate to Emma, but bequeathed his best horse to Beryl.

Beryl's memoir is our first source for the anecdotes of her life. Her childhood was not marked by birthdays or years, so I've taken the liberty of arranging the story in a way that makes sense to me. Although the tribe that raised her was Nandi, she often referred to them as Masai—a much fiercer tribe. Whenever I needed details about tribal customs, I used Masai references because there is much more research about the Masai compared to the Nandi.

The newspaper articles I quote are fictitious, but typical of the media coverage Beryl's exploit received. The quotes from her congratulatory telegrams are accurate. Beryl's reminiscences and story of her flight are based on her life, although the words are mine.

Beryl Markham died in Nairobi in 1986 at the age of 83. A memorial service was held for her in Kenya, fifty years to the day of her flight across the Atlantic.

FURTHER READING

There are several sources for information about Beryl and East Africa. I have listed some of the most useful.

Gourley, Catherine. *Beryl Markham: Never Turn Back*. Berkeley, CA: Conari Press, 1997.

Hollis, A.C. *The Masai: Their Language and Folklore*. Oxford: At the Clarendon Press, 1905.

Huxley, Elspeth. *The Flame Trees of Thika: Memories of an African Childhood*. New York: William Morrow, 1959.

Lovell, Mary. *Straight On Till Morning: The Biography of Beryl Markham*. New York: St. Martin's Press, 1987.

Maren, Michael. *The Land and People of Kenya*. New York: J.B. Lippincott, 1989.

Markham, Beryl. *West with the Night*. New York: North Point Press, 1983.

Markham, Beryl. *The Splendid Outcast*. New York: Farrar, Straus, Giroux, 1987.

Saitoti, Tepilit Ole. *The Worlds of a Maasai Warrior: An Autobiography*. New York: Random House, 1986.

Trzebinski, Errol. *The Lives of Beryl Markham*. New York: W.W. Norton & Co, 1993.

World Without Walls: Beryl Markham's African Memoir. (Audio) Van Nuys, CA: Wild Wing Productions, 1985.

ACKNOWLEDGMENTS

My mother, Barbara Burns, an amateur pilot and a fan of Beryl Markham's *West with the Night*, first suggested this story. While it was nerve-wracking (and eye-opening!) to hear about some of my mother's harrowing experiences, her insights about flying were invaluable.

My critique group's support was crucial—as it always is! Special thanks are due to Sari Bodi, Christine Pakkala, and Karen Swanson for their help in bringing Beryl's childhood to life.

Patricia Reilly Giff's generous advice inspired me to make sure that Beryl stayed true to herself without becoming a brat.

My agent George Nicholson found more depth in the novel than I knew was there and his wonderful assistant, Erica Rand Silverman, was a great help explaining contracts and other such arcane tidbits.

My editor at Chronicle Books, Victoria Rock, supported Beryl from the beginning and her deft edits brought the book to an entirely new and better place. The striking cover and clever interiors were designed by Jennifer Tolo Pierce. The marketing team, especially Lara Starr and Lea Yancey, have helped this new author understand how to sell a book and most importantly how to reach out to my readers.

My niece Madison and her mom, Anne Showalter, were beta readers—their faith in Beryl kept me going. Beryl's most infuriating and lovable characteristics can also be found in varying degrees in my beautiful daughters, Rowan and Margaux. And finally thank you to my husband, Rob, for his support and confidence.